Witch Stones

Lizzie Collins

ISBN 9798399653907

Acknowledgements

With thanks to Nova and Justin for their help
with the cover.
Your advice was much appreciated.

If you enjoy your journey through the story of the Grahams, Greenwoods and Elliots, I would be grateful if you would please leave a review on the Amazon Website.

Dear Reader.

Just a few words of explanation about this book.

This tale is set in a remote area of England, where the vernacular language is so ancient it would probably be understood by the Vikings.

I have included a bit, not a lot, of this speech for color and to add context to the story. For clarification, where this occurs I have added a note of explanation at the bottom of the page.

I hope you don't find it too distracting. If you do please feel free to email me at:

lizzie.collins.author@gmail.com

For ease of reading, pages 271 to 275 contain descriptions of characters and locations for reference.

The Life and Times of Claire Armstrong Graham as told by me, Meg Graham.

All my life I have been a child of nature. My father and uncle were lovers of animals, but as for myself, I needed to feel the nurturing earth beneath my feet and the warm green scent of growing things on the wind.

This story isn't mine but that of a lady by the name of Claire Armstrong Graham. Claire had a life touched by purest love and deepest tragedy. Her existence lurched from heartbreak to passion to a depression so deep it bordered on madness.

I am proud to say I was part of her pathway to happiness. It took a long time and involved some remarkable people, all of whom were nurtured by the land we farmed.

It wasn't an easy path either. It involved two murders - possibly three, I leave that to the reader to decide, for I was never sure myself. Claire was convinced she knew the truth. Perhaps she did. Perhaps Molly told her, although as my cousin Joe said: "Molly's a corpse and can't tell anybody anything."

Mary Carrick Graham, always known as Molly, was my grandmother and I wanted to believe in her, even though we never met.

All of us had good reason to pay respects to the Seven Sisters on their rocky mountain outcrop. The primordial maidens watched without speaking, judged without bias and played with all our lives as they saw fit.

I have recorded my own life with Claire's because, frankly, the two can't be untangled. Those she loved, I loved. Those she hated, were the bane of my life too, but although I knew dreadful poverty, I was never subjected to the pain she suffered.

My Aunt Claire was the bravest lady I ever knew and - along with a remarkable Irish turned Westmoreland harridan - the best friend I ever had.

Witch Stones

Chapter One

Death and Desertion

There were three of us Graham kids: our John, me Maggie, and the oldest Ellen of the big gob. The sod of it was she looked like Marilyn Monroe - boobs an' all .

She was a real beauty 'til she opened her mouth, which was like a sewer - except when Alan Mason was in earshot when she wiggled through Nethershaw. She had us all on tenterhooks in the hopes that one day she'd get caught out and Romeo would discover his Juliet was actually Ethel Merman in disguise.

Our mother had died just after John was born, leaving us with dad who preferred his sheep to his children. He spent all his time on the fells digging ewes out of ditches in the summer and snowdrifts in the winter, dipping them in disgusting antiseptic in the spring and hiring the sheerer.

Ellen's head was full of air, which left me to drag Johnny up. At least we could read and write - I'd hauled him with me the few miles down the hill to school on the odd days I went myself.

One day, dad didn't come home.

After near a week had gone by, by which time we'd finally noticed his absence, a search party from Nethershaw was called out and eventually they found him crushed beneath a ewe which had slipped down a scree slide and tumbled over and over, trapping him against a drystone wall.

Witch Stones

I was there when they brought his body down. He was a bit of a mess - head stoved in and arms and legs hanging at odd angles over the sides of the stretcher.

By the time of dad's death, Ellen was already apprenticed at the shoe factory and lived in a rented room in Kendal. She didn't much care anyway. As long as her petticoats were flounced and her lipstick the right shade of red, she didn't bother about much.

After our father had been buried and the bunch of flowers propped against the mound in the new grave-yard had turned to dust, Johnny came to tell me he'd joined the army. He'd have to do conscription so he might as well stay after, he said.

As John was only fifteen and there would be no responsible adult to sign any forms, I agreed to lie and forged dad's signature. The army weren't to know Robert Graham was six foot under I figured, and Johnny was only two years under age. Anyway, he'd the beginnings of a beard and Jacquie Leighton thought he looked like Ricky Nelson so he'd enough swagger about him to pass for seventeen.

Johnny was being picked up at the recruiting office in Kendal one Thursday afternoon. I did stir myself to see him off. He'd been shorn like one of dad's sheep and his uniform was too big, but he'd good boots and a kit bag with very little in it. He'd write, he said. He didn't but then neither did I.

Witch Stones

I was seventeen and left sitting in a two bedroomed crumbling ruin on the fells, euphemistically called Fairview. I had to think how to feed myself and pay the bills double-quick.

John's departure came as something of a relief although I was left with the sheep, which were beyond the abilities of a young girl to cope with.

Although he'd shown no interest in the Grahams before, Mr. Stoker from the next farm across took pity on me and sent his lad to give me a hand. He bought some of the better ewes and a good tup. The rest he helped take down to the auction mart in Nethershaw.

The beasts were shoved into pens, whilst I sat behind the iron rails in the ring as the auctioneer shouted the bidding in a language none but a sheep farmer would understand. I sat musing: how come sheep farmers smelled of cow's milk, and why did they tie their old wool coats shut with frayed twine?

Some of the local sheepmen diddled me and some were overly generous given my situation, so I reckon I about broke even.

I didn't sleep much that night waiting for the specter of my dad to come and haunt me for selling up. I suppose he must have had better things to do because he never showed.

Witch Stones

I tucked some of the money from my sales in the sock drawer and some in an old tea-caddy on the top shelf of the kitchen cupboard and went to look for a job.

Chapter Two

Valerie to the Rescue

As I walked through our little market town, the local schoolboys laughed at me, pulled my hair and told me I looked a 'scrow' - a mess - and to go take a look in a mirror. They were all younger than me - some even younger than John - and dead from the neck up. They were chased off by the school-master, Mr. Richardson.

"You look to your own affairs or there'll be extra work at home-time tomorrow," he promised, his voice deceptively quiet.

"Come child," Mr. Richardson said to me. "We'll go sit with my sister and see if we can't find some solution to your problems."

I'd done what the village boys said and gone home and looked in a mirror. They were right - I did look a 'scrow'. We took a bath once a month in front of the fire but since dad had gone I hadn't bothered too much. I just gave myself an 'up and a downer' in a bowl of cold water with the edge taken off with scalding from the kettle. There was always plenty of sheep lanolin for soap which was great for my skin but stank awful.

I did the best I could with my appearance and with Miss Richardson's help, found employment at Luneside House, home of gentleman farmer and local magistrate, Mr. Mitford-Clarke.

Witch Stones

I turned up at his back door none too fragrant, with my meager belongings tied up in an old tablecloth.

The housekeeper looked me up and down and led me to a little room off the kitchen with a bed and a dresser.

"Drop your things on the floor - you can sort them later. For the present, I'll draw you a bath - you smell like a farmyard."

"You've got nits," she announced and gave me a tub of powder and a fine-toothed comb.

"Rub some of that in, wait ten minutes then hop in the bath, wash your hair and comb it out. You'll have to do it again tomorrow and the day after. Perhaps Matt can find you some jobs in the garden until you're clean. You're not to mix with anyone else in this house until I say, do you understand me?"

I followed her instructions and was surprised at how many little black dots appeared on the surface of the bath-water. I'd always itched a bit but hadn't given it much thought.

When my hair hadn't come clean in three days, Miss Dent - that was the housekeeper's name - took the kitchen scissors and lopped it off. I was mortified. I looked like an elf! I had a tiny little nose, high cheekbones and a pointy chin. What was even more depressing was I was as flat as a pancake. I looked like a model for Disney's Peter Pan and gazed at Miss Dent my eyes like saucers. She stood behind me, the remains of my hair dangling from her fist and a blank expression on her face.

"Go wash it again - and put all your things in the dustbin. I'll see if Miss Jennifer has some old clothes that'll fit."

Witch Stones

Jennifer was Jennifer Mitford-Clarke, daughter of the house. Because of the vermin problem we hadn't bumped into each other at Luneside, although I had seen her around at school. We kids were all lumped together through junior school before being syphoned off to Kendal Grammar or Secondary Mod. If like me your parents needed you for work, you left unofficially at thirteen and that was that.

Jenny was very popular and always wore a green velvet hairband and Mary Jane shoes. I was the other end of the scale. My hair - before Miss Dent's ministrations - had always been held back with a hairgrip and my shoes were hand-me-downs - Ellen's or Johnny's depending on which were in best repair at the time.

When we finally met, I was introduced by Miss Dent as I tried on one of Jenny's old frocks. She was a normal shape for a seventeen year old whereas..... well, I wasn't. Miss Dent was sticking pins in the dress all over in an attempt to make it fit. Eventually it did - after a fashion.

"I'm sorry," I said to Mrs. Mitford-Clarke.

What the hell for, I couldn't later imagine. It may just have been that Miss Dent was butchering one of Jenny's [1]Marks and Sparks dresses on my behalf.

"You have her measurements now," said Mrs. Mitford-Clarke. "Do the blue striped and the grey one with the

[1]*Marks and Spencers - a good quality clothes store*

7

pearl buttons and lace collar as well. How are you for underwear, Maggie?"

Did she mean knickers and vests? I'd never had any, nor socks neither. Without waiting for an answer she rattled on:

"Perhaps we should think about your name as well. Maggie sounds like a sheepdog. Daisy? You don't like that?" she asked, noticing the look of dismay on my face.

I didn't. We'd once had a cow called Daisy dad kept for milk when we were small. She had constant diarrhea.

"What about Meg - like in 'Little Women'?"

I nodded enthusiastically. Mr. Richardson had read that to us in school. Meg was very grown up and responsible.

"Now then, we'll take a walk into town this afternoon and buy you some knickers and socks. You haven't put her in that awful old pantry off the kitchen were we put the sheerers, have you Miss Dent?"

"It was just until we'd deloused her, Madam. I didn't intend it to be a permanent arrangement."

"Put her in Jane Dinsdale's old room."

Mrs. Mitford-Clarke turned to me:

"It's small and in the attic but it's quite comfortable."

I thanked her and dropped a curtsey.

"No need for that, dear," she said.

Chapter Three

Jennifer Moves On

I was very fortunate that Jenny and I took to each other straight away - I don't think she could have remembered me from school.

Without conscious decision by anyone, I'd moved from servitude to companion to a young lady of quality. At Jenny's insistence, I'd been moved into the room next to hers which had ceilings ten feet tall and a bed-quilt.

When I'd arrived at Luneside House, Jenny was already at the Girls' Grammar in Kendal and my occasional school days had been over for some years.

Since I lacked a home of my own and the family had been so kind to me, I gave all my attention to my work as a general servant. I was included in everything - picnics on the lawn, swimming in the river and long rambles round nearby lakes. It was a world away from Fairview.

A couple of years later, when I'd managed belatedly to grow a few modest curves, and decided to keep my Peter Pan hair in a largely failed attempt to imitate Audrey Hepburn, Jenny came to my room and sat on the bed looking depressed.

"They want me to go to University in Manchester. MAN-CHESTER!" she said in despair.

Jen was appalled when she realized we couldn't continue as we always had, so she stamped her kitten-heels and begged Daddy to do something. When that didn't work she point blank refused the university course in English

Literature and said she'd buy my old hill farm and raise
sheep. I nearly died laughing. Sheep were to Jennifer
what Mickey Mouse was to her Lit. course. Finally Mr.
Mitford-Clarke gave in and promised if she took up her
studies in Manchester, he'd find me a job and we could
still see each other in the holidays.

Jen now knew her fate, but I'd to await mine still. It was
nerve wracking but eventually it was decided I might be
able to make myself useful around my boss's office or
failing that, Matt Elliot the gardener, who I knew well by
this point, might find me some light work.

On rare occasions, I walked up into the hills to check on
my old home. The passage of time had made it more and
more dilapidated. I doubted the kitchen fire would catch
alight now. It was so long since it'd been used that damp
had seeped down the chimney. The whole place smelled
of wet soot.

I thought about selling it, but who would want the bloody
thing? It was well-nigh derelict. The sale of the grazing
land on the fells, together with the money from the auc-
tioned sheep, which I had so carefully hidden away, came
to quite a tidy sum, but the doors and windows were becoming increasingly rotten and insecure. Rather than having my treasure pinched by some passing tramp, I made
the effort to slog uphill through driving rain to retrieve the
cash I'd so carefully hidden. Mr. Mitford-Clarke helped
me open an account at his bank. I was becoming a woman
of substance.

I suppose it was inevitable that now our paths had parted
so completely, Jenny and I began to lose touch.

Chapter Four

Independence and a Disappearance

Having been on the nasty end of extreme poverty I decided to solve my problems by putting some of my savings into buying a small market garden further down the valley from Nethershaw, where the soil was richer and easier to manage.

Jenny's father lent me Matt Elliot his gardener, to help me get started.

Matt was a quiet man, who felt the warmth of the sun in the soil and coaxed forth the most amazing flowers and vegetables. He walked away with prize after prize at the local shows for his exquisite dahlias.

As I wanted to learn how to support myself on the proceeds from my garden, dahlias were not a priority. I needed vegetables. So we planted potatoes, carrots and leeks in neatly hoed rows and trained cucumbers and beautiful scarlet-flowered beans over trellises. My produce sold well at the Wednesday Farmers' Market.

Then I bought a few hens. The eggs were delicious but I loathed wringing their necks, plucking and gutting them. The goddamn things just wouldn't stay dead. I once watched one run round a hutch for a full fifteen minutes before it dropped on its back with its feet in the air.

Matt came over to help when he had the time. Between us we built a shed of caulked planks, and when the weather allowed, we would sit in the sunshine in silence since we were usually too knackered to speak. Come to think of it,

Matt did everything in silence. He rarely opened his mouth at all.

Once we had the shed, we fixed guttering to the roof and piped rain water into a huge lidded butt. That saved many hours hauling water from a spring on the edge of the site.

Then Matt just disappeared and when he hadn't turned up for the best part of a week I began to wonder why.

I went to Luneside House, but Mr. Mitford-Clarke hadn't seen him either. He was annoyed and had gone so far as to prepare Matt's outstanding wages and tax forms to be handed over when, and if, he finally turned up.

But he didn't.

He seemed to have disappeared off the face of the earth. Matthew had two aunts in the town but they had no idea where he was either.

Once the garden took off, I'd moved out of Luneside House and now had a pokey little apartment above the Yorkshire Penny Bank on Main Street. Jen sometimes stayed with me when she came home. Her University pals would come with her occasionally. I didn't care much for them. They were loud, self-opinionated and rude. Once, one of them sneered at a local farmer's lad and called him a 'bumpkin' when he accidentally blocked his way to the bar. The black eye he got meant they didn't come round so often after that, which was a relief.

Jenny chose to stay away with them too, a sadness both to me and her parents.

Chapter Five

An Autopsy in Kendal

Over time, my modest business thrived, and I had unwittingly become a farmer again - only not bloody sheep, thank the Lord.

First I bought a two acre field which produced a bumper crop thanks to help from Dan Barber, Tony Scar and some lads from the town I employed as occasional labor.

Eventually Tony sloped off to pastures new, so I converted an old ruined barn as a home for Dan and his family in an effort to keep a permanent worker.

The following year's crop surplus produced enough money to rent a further eight acres which I later bought. It was one hell of a lot of hard slog but I was now the proud owner of a dilapidated eighteenth century farmhouse called Ghyll Howe.

You can grow tons of potatoes, carrots and leeks on ten acres and I was able to invest in a second-hand potato harvester, several tractors with trailers, and built barns for storage.

I sold to shops and businesses - first to Kendal and local markets - then as far away as Leeds and Harrogate.

I abandoned the little allotment where I'd begun, and with

Dan and Tony Scarr who [1]I'd slipped a few quid on the lump, went to dismantle the last bits and pieces of equipm ent. We disassembled the guttering which had dropped

[1]*paid a few pounds cash (usually to avoid tax).*

off the roof, took down the shed and burned it and the trellising, but when we came to shift the water barrel it took all three of us to move it.

I couldn't think why. I'd never tried moving it before, even though I'd been syphoning off water from the tap before I shut the place down. It shouldn't have been that heavy, especially since the guttering which fed it lay in pieces on the ground.

Dan pulled off the lid, recoiled by several yards and sat on his arse in a patch of nettles, his face contorted in horror.

I leaned over and took a look. At first I saw just a grey glutinous mass, but then in the part closest to the surface I noticed the outline of a boot.

I slapped the lid back on, sent the lads back to Ghyll Howe on the pretext of eating, then drove like a lunatic to fetch Constable Ryder. He took one look, said, 'fucking hell!' and went to find Mr. Mitford-Clarke who as magistrate was the nearest thing we had to a coroner. The last murder in Nethershaw was probably when they burned a witch in the seventeenth century.

Mr. Mitford-Clark arrived with our one and only town doctor, rang Kendal hospital and instructed the medical examiner and proper Coroner to meet him - or more accurately the four of us - at the hospital morgue as soon as possible after the hour it took us to get there. Mr. Mitford-Clarke drove himself and arranged to meet us at the hospital.

The medical examiner said submerged bodies decompose slower than ones subjected to the air so it would be helpful if we could take the whole [1]kit and kaboodle to the hospital for examination. So I recalled my lads, hoisted the water butt onto the back of a trailer and secured it good and tight with ropes.

Nethershaw's doctor, a potato farmer and our entourage sat in the back of the trailer glancing nervously at the barrel every time we went over a bump in the road.

We dropped off our load at the hospital, then we all went back to Nethershaw, except for poor Mr. Mitford-Clarke who had to hang around for the identification.

I went home, threw up and went to bed where I dreamed of murder and bloated bodies bobbing about in barrels.

One thing was apparent - he sure as hell hadn't committed suicide.

[1]*everything*

Chapter Six

Hugo's Horror

I had begun my day by totting up some numbers at the kitchen table, while I drank my morning cuppa and did my best not to remember the happenings of the previous twenty-four hours.

It was a beautiful morning, still misty from dawn, with the aroma of freshly turned soil in the air. Both would disappear with the rising of the sun, so I went outside and leaned against the barn wall to enjoy the serenity before it melted away.

Mr. Mitford-Clarke skidded his Jag into my yard. He got out banging the door, which skittered the few chickens I still kept, into a dither of clucking.

"Put the kettle on, there's a good girl. You'd better fill your own cup too - you're going to need it."

I pushed my accounts aside and sat him at the kitchen table. He put his elbows on the oilcloth covering and shook his head.

"The body was complete, although given the passage of time, concertinaed. They asked me to stay in case there were identifiable marks. "

"Did you know who it was? Was it somebody you recognized?"

He'd been slowly recovering his color, but at my question his complexion became waxen again and he rubbed his hands over his face.

"Matt."

Oh, bloody hell! I'd sat on my folding chair next to the water barrel for months after he disappeared and never knew. I'd even watered my vegetables, filling my can from the barrel's tap without realizing.

On reflection, the water did seem to come out slowly and once or twice I'd poked a piece of garden cane up it to get it going. Oh… my…. God!

"Are you sure? If he was badly decomposed you could have made a mistake. Lots of laborers round here are about the same shape and size."

"It was him - I'm quite positive. The body had no identifying marks but he's the only person hereabouts whose gone missing for years."

That sounded more like an opinion than a positive fact to me, but then I hadn't been at the autopsy.

Much to my dismay, he put his head in his hands, shoulders shaking. This was my former boss, my friend's father and the local Magistrate. This man was gentry to be looked up to.

"It's a lot to ask Meg, but would you come with me to see Matt's aunts?"

Suffice to say, our visit to the Misses Elliot was not a happy one. They were quite stoic for a while, pleased for the closure, but began to weep and wail when Mr. Mitford-Clarke said:

"I would advise you not to view the body. Pick out a casket and I'll arrange for Matthew to be placed inside and the lid screwed shut."

I was sure that could have been put more delicately, but perhaps it was best done quick.

Their first reaction was to go to chapel to pray. They asked that we accompany them, but Mr. Mitford-Clarke cried off, saying he had urgent business to attend to, but short of pleading the harvesting of spuds, there wasn't a lot I could say.

So I went.

Chapter Seven

A Wedding and a Funeral

Nethershaw Primitive Methodist Chapel was typical of its type: a double door led to a small foyer housing a table with a stack of hymn books. The body of the chapel smelt of the odd mixture of dust and beeswax peculiar to places of worship, and the scent of lilac some devoted matron had arranged on every windowsill.

Apart from my dad's funeral and the occasional carol service, I'd never darkened the door of a house of the Almighty in my life; nor had a parson ever managed to climb the hill to our farm.

Ruth and Marjorie - best described as 'grey' - hair, skin, eyes and clothes - led me, one on each side, straight down one of the two aisles to a door beside a pulpit. Door, floor, pulpit and pews were polished to a remarkable degree.

The two ladies banged arbitrarily on the door and strode straight in without waiting for a by-your-leave. The minister had just pulled up his pants and was fastening his belt.

Rather than be irritated by the interruption, he grinned at the Salem witches at my side and said:

"And how're my beautiful girls this fine day?"

Although they'd come to arrange their nephew's burial, they both tittered coyly.

The minister came as a bit of a surprise. He stuck out his hand and shook mine warmly.

"Tim Robertshaw at your service. Very glad to see a new face around here - not that the old ones aren't a vision to behold."

It was all I could do to keep a straight face. This was a clever man. He'd managed to make two elderly ladies feel like Doris Day, while calling them old in the same sentence.

The Misses Elliot began solemnly to discuss arrangements for the funeral of their nephew, with their friend the minister.

It being a Thursday afternoon, I assumed he'd have a fair bit of time to spare. My limited experience led me to suppose clergymen only worked one day a week - perhaps two if you take into account time to write the sermon and pick the hymns. I supposed he'd to find time for weddings and funerals too... and the occasional Christening. Observing the three of them with their heads together over service sheets, perhaps he'd be busier than I thought,

"Good day to you Miss...?"

"Graham, Margaret Graham," I replied using - appropriately - my Sunday name.

"Oh, yes. Meg Graham. I know of your sister through Mr. Lacey of Kendal Methodists."

'ELLEN?'

He must have noted the expression on my face because he said:

"You weren't at the wedding? Perhaps you went to 'The Lamb and Staff' afterwards?"

WEDDING! I only lived fifteen miles up the bloody road. She could have let me know, the cow. I strode from the chapel fuming and went in a temper to skim stones across the river.

So who had Ellen married? Once I'd calmed down I was consumed with curiosity. I'd have to go back and see the minister.

By the time I'd returned, the ladies had left, and Mr. Robertshaw was sliding hymn numbers into their frame. As I entered, he smiled.

"I take it you didn't know about the wedding."

"No I didn't. I don't know why I was so mad. We haven't seen each other in years. There's three of us and we're not what you'd call close - never have been. Our brother Johnny's in the army and I've no idea where he is either. Last I heard, Ellen was in Kendal working at the shoe factory. Who's she married?"

"Jonathan Mackie, I believe his name is."

Jonathan Mackie? And as reality dawned:

"Are you sure? Mackie's the name of the boss at 'Lonsdale Shoes'."

"I believe it's his son. You really are out of touch - you could walk to Kendal on a good day from here."

"We were all stuck together in a sheep farm half way up Aidafell for the first fifteen years of our lives. None of us got on - it was purgatory."

"Hope of redemption then," said the minister and grinned.

"I'm more concerned about Matt Elliot and his aunts for now," I said shortly. "Mr. Mitford-Clarke's in Court this afternoon, so I'll have to stand in his stead."

"Before we continue, can I ask you to please call me Tim? 'Reverend' and 'minister' are so…. religious. A lot of the older folks in the town cling to the title. If it gives them comfort then fine, but it does grate."

"Okay. What about the funeral? Is there anything I can do? Do you know if the ladies can afford the undertaker?"

The end result was that the two old girls had a fair bit of cash squirrelled away so there were no problems.   Mr. Mitford-Clarke picked up the shortfall which wasn't much.

Matt was buried next to the church wall with a headstone the text of which read:

Here lies Matt Elliot
Planted like his Dahlias

"The Church frowns on humor in death - but what the hell! If you can't laugh it becomes serious," shrugged Tim Robertshaw. "Ruth said it's what Matt would have wanted and her opinion trumps the bishop's any day."

Chapter Eight

A Confusion of Communication

The period between the discovery of a death and the burial is the worst for the grieving. It's as if the deceased hovers half-way between this world and the next.

Whilst the Misses Elliot were burying their nephew, there remained the problem of the perpetrator. Constable Ryder was mostly experienced in pub brawls and poaching.

I happened to call into the Lion the afternoon he greeted Inspector Fernside from Penrith CID, and they were discussing the case over a pint.

"This is Miss Margaret Graham, sir. The body was found on her allotment," began Bob Ryder.

The Inspector fixed me with an eagle eye, assessing me as a suspect I supposed. Then, apparently dismissing me as a murderer - probably because I was five foot four with a face like a pixie - he smiled, sat back and lit his pipe.

"And a good day to you Miss Graham. I shall be compiling a list of people for questioning. I will see your name's at the top. Today, you'll appreciate I need to find my digs and settle in. I'll call you in the morning with a time."

"I'm afraid that's not possible," I said. "I'm going to Skipton on business but I'll be available at your convenience Saturday."

I thought the inspector was about to blow a gasket.

"You don't seem to appreciate the seriousness of the situation Miss Graham. I'll see you tomorrow."

"Inspector Fernside, Matt has been dead for so long even his own aunts are forgetting him, and by now the murderers might be in Timbuktu. I don't see that one day would make any difference."

He puffed out his chest like a pigeon at this assault on his dignity and turned red in the face.

"I will see you in the morning, Miss Graham," he insisted.

"I'm afraid you'll be waiting in vain, Inspector. Better call number two on your list - I have a business to run."

I caught a glance of Bob Ryder hiding a grin behind his beer glass as I walked to the door.

I *did* go to Skipton and the inspector *did* call number two on his list, who happened to be Tony Scarr who'd helped shift the barrel.

I had this report from 'Bobby' Ryder in the pub that evening. He said he'd have paid good money to see it over again and had unusually recorded it word for word in his notepad.

Tony Scarr was a true man of Westmoreland who didn't mince his words, as PC Ryder was to relate. He flipped over the pages of his book.

The inspector's first question was, in true Poirot fashion:

"What were you doing on the morning of August 4th 1955, Mr. Scarr?"

Tony removed his cap, scratched his head and said:

Witch Stones

[1]"Well lad. I were nobbut kallin wi' Miss Graham. Then 'er other man - Dan Barber, weren't it Bob? - raised t'lid on't watter butt an' all 'ell were let loose."

"You will speak proper English, man, or I will have you arrested!"

Tony looked at him blankly:

[2]"But I were, lad. Best I know 'ow. Don't let 'im put me in t'slammer Bob!"

Mr. Fernside muttered something along the lines of 'oh, shit' and waved him out.

Tony bowed his head and got out while the going was good.

By the time Bob had finished his account we had tears of laughter running down our cheeks. I said a prayer for forgiveness to Matt but guessed he'd have seen the funny side of it. Inspector Fernside's life was going to be hell for the rest of the investigation.

As Bob was reading, Tim Robertshaw had quietly pulled out a chair and sat down, just about choking on his beer as the story unfolded.

"Bet Matt enjoyed that!" he said, evidently thinking along the same lines as me. "Who's on tomorrow?"
"I am," I groaned, "for my sins."

[1]*"Well sir, I was chatting to Miss Graham when her other man, Dan Barber, wasn't it Bob? - lifted the lid on the water butt and all hell was let loose"*

[2]*But I was, Sir. Best I know how. Don't let him put me in jail, Bob."*

"I'll try and think of an excuse to be there. Absolution?"

"Who for? Me or him."

"Remains to be seen, I suppose."

The three of us drank to that, and the landlord smirked as he dried glasses behind the bar.

Chapter Nine

'Ello, 'ello, 'ello - What's All This Then?

I was up for questioning at ten sharp the following morning.

I'd been working in the fields since dawn so turned up in overalls and gumboots. It was evident from his expression the Inspector thought I could have made more effort with my appearance.

"Good morning, Inspector Fernside," I said holding my hand out to shake.

"And to you Miss Graham," he said sourly without looking up from his notes.

[1]"Reet cracker of a mornin'."

I just couldn't resist it and was very gratified to see him stiffen.

I recounted the events of that day as closely as I could, leaving out none of the gruesome details. When he'd finished his questions, Mr. Fearnside deigned to shake my hand and PC Ryder showed me out.

"He's questioning people in the order they found out about it." said Bob after the door had closed. "God alone knows what he'll do when he hits the town gossips. He won't understand a word and they'll be harder to shut up than Tony by a mile. Its's Dan Barber in t'morning, then he's going over to Luneside to see t'Magistrate in t'after-noon."

"I'd a phone call a couple of days ago from a distant

[1] *Beautiful morning*

27

cousin I haven't seen in donkey's years, I've to go to Beckton Monday to pay him a visit. For some reason best known to himself, he wants to take on Fairview. He'll likely have Catherine Earnshaw banging at his windows."

Bob looked at me blankly so I said:

"You know.... Catherine Earnshaw... 'Wuthering Heights'?" I looked heavenwards. "Emily Bronte?"

He shrugged. He clearly had no idea what I was talking about so I

changed the subject.

"I'm looking forward to that drive like a hole in the head. I just hope this bloody weather cheers up. It's a choice of sixty miles of good roads via Kendal, which'll take most of the day or forty miles over the tops. Quicker, but you could lose a hay wagon in some of the pot-holes.

"Tell his Godship I won't be available until Thursday."

I hurried off home as I wanted to see Dan Barber before his interrogation the following day.

He was the closest I had at that time to a farm manager, and the only lad who lived on the farm. The cottage I'd had renovated was at the far end of our eight acre field, so his twins could make as much noise as they wanted. They were the only kids I ever knew who could scare the shit out of geese. Of course he hadn't known them when he called one Angelique - Anj- and the other John-Claude. I'd have loved to be a fly on the wall on the boy's first day at Nethershaw National school toting a name like that.

Witch Stones

I could never remember Mrs. Barber's name. Until they carved it on the tomb-stone, I always thought of her as 't'wife'.

I tripped over a [1]trike on its side as I walked up the path. It was red, scratched and the chain was hanging off.

"Wot you want?" said a child's voice as I was about to bang on the door.

I turned to see a small girl with unruly curls and a snotty nose standing behind me. Strangely, apart from the nose, she looked remarkably well scrubbed, but crumpled.

"Is your Dad in? I need to speak to him."

"You're t'boss-lady, in't you?" chimed in a voice from behind her. "Dad

says if we don't behave, you'll send us to [1]t'norfnidge." He looked

puzzled. [2]"Wot's a norfnidge?"

"Where's your Dad? I need to speak to him," I reiterated, patience fast wearing thin.

[3]"'e's in t'scullery - come for 'is snap."

I banged on the door, and as footsteps approached Tweedle Dee and Tweedle Dumb disappeared round the side of the house.

A be-aproned Mrs. Dan opened the door looking bellige

[1]*tricycle - child's three-wheeled bike*
[2]*orphanage*
[3]*He's in the kitchen - come for his lunch*

-rent until she took note of who I was, then she bellowed:

"Daniel - it's f'thee," and disappeared into the dim interior.

"Oh, 'ello, Miss Graham. Come in…"

"No thanks. I've to go to Beckton Monday. I'll be gone a few days. I'm just here to warn you Policeman Plod - the detective from Penrith - is on the warpath and you're next in line of fire at ten oclock in the morning. Be at the 'station on time in your [2]best bib and tucker. It's about Matt. He just wants your account of what you saw. Do your best to make it in English, Tony Scarr baffled him no end - he wasn't happy."

Dan looked nervous.

"Nothing to worry about. Just tell him the truth. We'd all like to know what happened."

He nodded.

"Well, good-day Miss. When will you be back? It's wages Friday."

"I should be back by then. I'm placing a deal of trust in you Dan, but I'll make it worth your while, especially if your wife does dinner for the rest of them and sees to the hens."

There was a loud huff from behind him as he shut the door.

"So what *is* a bloody norfnidge anyway," said twin two to twin one as I banged the gate shut behind me.

[1]*best clothes*

Chapter Ten

Joseph Graham and the Beckton Wiggle.

I drove to Beckton the long way round after all. The last time I'd taken the other route, I'd run out of petrol on Aidafell and ended up sleeping in the car - not an experience I'd care to repeat.

The cousin wasn't distant except in acquaintance. He was my dad's brother's son, but as neither of our fathers had spoken for years, I'd never met Joseph Graham before.

Fearing the family feud might have come down the generations, I'd thought to book into a B&B before I left. I arrived at 'Valley View' at eight o'clock that evening, to be greeted by a typical northern guest-house owner. She opened the door having clearly just whipped off her wraparound pinny and flung it over the back of the nearest chair.

Mrs. Mattison showed me into a very comfy room with a feather bed with a candlewick bedspread.

"I dare say you could use a cup o' tea," she said, on her way out of the door. It was delivered on a tray with a starched hand-embroidered cloth. "Breakfast's nine o'clock sharp. Bathroom's down the 'all," she called from the dog-leg on the stairs.

The following morning, I rang my cousin from an old-fashioned wall-telephone in the family parlor, with Mrs. Mattison and her husband looking expectantly on. At a meaningful stare from Mr. Mattison, when I'd finished, I left two pennies in a box with 'Telephone Money' taped clearly to one side.

My cousin and I arranged to meet that lunchtime on neutral ground in Beckton's one and only pub. It was a lovely old-fashioned place with the unusual name of 'The Pick and Shovel'. It had watercolors of local beauty spots on the walls, and horse-brasses over the fireplace.

I ordered a half and sat down to wait.

The door opened repeatedly after that. Most were locals greeted by the landlord.

A couple walked in, looked round then walked out again only to return five minutes later.

The man was tall, very well dressed and perhaps a few years younger than me. His companion was... well... gorgeous. She had naturally blonde hair, unusual brown eyes and had a wiggle Ellen would have died for.

She hitched herself onto a bar stool, one cheek on and one off and ordered a 'Cuba Libre', then told the perplexed landlord who was more used to orders of bitter and lager and lime:

"Silly! (titter), it's only a rum and Coca Cola (giggle)."

I was so fascinated by the exchange, I almost missed what her boyfriend said to me,

"Good evening. Are you by chance Margaret Graham... from Nethershaw? I'm supposed to meet her here, and you're the only unaccompanied lady."

I stood abruptly, bumping the table and knocking my fortunately empty glass over.

"Are *you* Joseph Graham?"

I tried unsuccessfully to keep the incredulity out of my voice.

"Joe. I am," he shook my hand and smiled.

"I'm delighted to meet you, May I buy you a drink?"

"Yes, Thank you."

While he was at the bar, 'Mae West' tottered over and introduced herself.

"So you're little Meggie. Joe talks about you all the time (titter)."

Not likely since we'd never met.

"My name is Margaret Graham and you are…. ?"

"Marilyn," wouldn't she just be. "Marilyn Lumb."

"Mary…. " smiled Joseph, sticking pins in her balloon. "I see you've met my cousin."

"Yes," said 'Monroe', looking with distain at my callused hands as I took the glass from her boyfriend. She tossed blonde curls and pouted.

"See you later Honey. Don't be long."

She gave me the grimace of a smile, tossed her jacket over her shoulder and slouched through the door to the tap-room.

"Don't mind her," said Joe as she disappeared. "To tell the truth, I was nervous as hell about meeting you so I rang round for a date. She was the only one free on such short notice."

He appeared to be a well-educated and prosperous man, immaculately dressed, with capable well-manicured hands. This was a Graham? What the hell did he want with Fairview?

"Where shall we begin?" he asked, raising his shoulders.

"Well, at the beginning, I suppose."

"Right. I'm twenty-two years old. I work with my dad who owns Bythwaite Farm about five miles up the valley; sheep mostly but some arable - wheat, hay for winter feed. Your father was a sheep farmer too, wasn't he?"

"I'm Margaret - Meg - Graham And yes, he was a hill farmer until the sheep took over. One of them crushed him against a wall."

Oh, Lord, that said far more than I meant to share with a stranger, even if he was family.

"Yes, so I understand."

He looked politely regretful,

"And you, what do you do? That I don't know."

I explained my situation and he looked suitably impressed, which was nice of him.

"From a standing start I'm not doing too badly. Got problems at the moment but they'll resolve themselves.

"You come as something of a relief from the last of my new acquaintances - an inept police inspector they've sent from Penrith to investigate a body on an allotment I own. He managed in two days to offend half of Nethershaw. I'm glad to be out of Inspector Fearnside's reach for a while."

He looked intrigued then laughed and said:

"Thanks a lot! One step up from a lousy copper has to be an improvement on what my dad thinks of me. Want to talk about it?"

"I absolutely do not," I said emphatically.

Chapter Eleven

The Brothers Ying and Yang

Thankfully, the 'blonde bombshell' lived in the village so Joe could walk her home. I locked my own car and waited for him at his Austin Healey in the pub car park.

He must have been nervous because he crashed the gears as he pulled out onto the road and said:

"It's only a short drive and I have to explain about my father. He tends to be ….." He searched for an appropriate word and came up with "…. irascible."

Bad-tempered old bastard then. That didn't bode well. I wasn't known for my tact.

"I'm sure we'll get along just fine."

"He's not a bad old stick but it's important you know what comes out of his mouth is not always what's in his head."

I changed the subject.

"What's your interest in Fairview?"

"Forgive me, but can we postpone that discussion until you meet Dad?"

I had no time to answer because before the words were out of his mouth we'd pulled off the road into Bythwaite's neat and orderly farmyard.

As we neared the door it was opened by a plump girl with braids and a starched apron.

"Hello Joe, I've not put the kettle on yet."

"Mr. Joe, Sarah. You've a memory like a sieve. And you always address the lady first."

"Sorry Joe. What's your name Miss?"

"Meg … Meg Graham." I replied.

"Glad to know you. You can't be called Graham. These here are Grahams," she said, her gesture encompassing the entire house.

"Miss Meg's dad and Mr. Graham were brothers," explained my cousin.

"Likely that makes you related then," she said and disappeared indoors.

Joe took my jacket and hung in on a hook in the coatroom, above upturned Wellingtons on a rack. In a lowered voice he explained:

"Sarah's been a boon to my mother. She's been failing recently - she suffers from dementia. Dad can't be bothered with the day to day running of the house so we employed Sarah's mother as house-keeper as well but she comes in from the village."

"Sit in here," he said, showing me into a room with pretty chintz covers on the furniture. "I'll organize some tea. Dad's out by the looks of things so we'll have a bit of peace and quiet for a while."

Not hopeful at all.

He left, I assumed to arrange refreshments, so I made myself comfortable in an armchair next to the fireplace. When he returned I said:

"Do you know why our fathers fell out? Was there a particular reason or did they just grow apart? Nethershaw's a long distance to move away."

"I don't know precisely why. I can only tell you Bythwaite Farm is the family home and your father grew up here. He was the younger brother - always his mother's baby. There was probably a fair bit of jealousy involved and it must have been one hell of a blow up to put my uncle in such a remote croft so far from his family."

"It's not a croft," I corrected him. "I own it - it's a small-holding."

I was interrupted by the slamming of an outside door and a deep voice bellowed:

"Joseph - you there? There's tools in the back of the Land Rover. I need help shifting them."

A small tough-looking man with tanned skin and aggressive stance, who I took to be Richard Graham my dad's brother, had kicked off his boots and stood in the doorway in his stocking feet, still clad in a waxed jacket.

"Who's this?" he asked dismissively over the top of my head. I was getting less confident by the minute.

"This is Uncle Robert's daughter Meg – Meg Graham."

"Robert's girl? What's she want?"

I stuck out my hand which my uncle pointedly ignored.

"You asked me to call - at least your manager did. So here I am." I said brightly.

He turned to Joe.

"Remind me. What did we want with her?"

"You wanted to buy her Fairview small-holding at Nethershaw."

"Ah yes. Changed my mind."

He pulled on his wellies again and left. I watched him climb into his Land Rover, tools and me evidently forgotten. Joe looked as if he wished the ground would open up and swallow him.

"Well," I said, "I don't think 'irascible' quite covered that, do you? And before you say anything further, it's not your fault so don't you even think of apologizing."

"How about I buy Fairview myself? I've been looking for a project," said Joe.

Chapter Twelve

Malice

Joe had handed me into his Healey, ready to drive to the village when his father swerved back into the yard. He screeched to a halt, jumped out and banged the door shut with such force it flew open again. Elbowing Joe out of the way and ramming his face into mine, he ground out:

"That bastard's runt are you? Get your arse off my property."

Then to my utter astonishment, he burst into tears, strode off to his vehicle and took off across the yard as if all the demons in hell were after him.

I turned and looked at Joe, eyes wide, mouth agape and totally speechless.

"Past opening time," he said.

We were back at the pub within half an hour.

"What happened?" I asked, aghast. "He sounded unhinged - he seemed to behave oddly after you mentioned Fairview. Why *do* you want to buy it? It must be years since I was there and to the best of my knowledge Johnny's still defending Queen and Country. Ellen won't have been - she loathes the place.

"I've to go back to Nethershaw tomorrow to try and straighten out this mess with Matt, and to see Dan Barber about the farm. He's my fill-in foreman and a good worker but not Brain of Britain, so I daren't leave him any longer. It's a shame this has been such a wild goose chase."

"Dan doesn't manage your farm then?" he asked,

"He does in a way, I suppose. The truth of the matter is I can grow best quality crops, but my man-management skills are sadly lacking. I've had to learn as I've gone along."

"Would you like me to come with you? I can check out Fairview at the same time. The old man can't object to that."

But object he did, much to Joe's mortification, so I ended up driving back to Nethershaw alone.

When I got back home, all hell had broken loose - Fearnside had arrested Dan. He was clearly frustrated he hadn't been able to contact me, but as I only intended being away a couple of days I hadn't seen the need to leave details.

Detective Inspector Fearnside was not of the same opinion. It must have been an act of pure malice to arrest Dan Barber for the murder - he couldn't even warm his own kid's arses.

If that dick Fearnside couldn't get to the bottom of this, and if I could stay out of clink myself, then I'd have to do my own investigating.

Chapter Thirteen

Dan Barber [1]'Banged Up'

I cleaned my shoes and put on my best frock as I intended visiting Luneside House. I drove round Back Lane to avoid the police station and prayed Fearnside wasn't looking out of the window as I drove past his digs.

The door was opened by Mrs. Mitford-Clarke. She'd been planting begonias so for once had more soil on her than I did.

"How lovely to see you Meg. Come and have some lemonade. Miss Dent has just put a jug in the conservatory."

She was a reserved person but had always been kind to me. As she was viewed with deference by those who'd taken it upon themselves to impose their opinions on the rest of Nethershaw, she didn't have much company. I realized with shame I was guilty of not calling on her as often as I should. I'd put that right once I'd extricated myself from this fiasco.

With that in mind, I spent half an hour in inconsequential chatter, mostly about Jen who after her graduation was living in Toronto with some school teacher her mother didn't approve of. Although she'd an expensive engagement ring, he was prevaricating over the date said Valerie. Or Jennifer was, I thought cynically.

Mrs. Mitford-Clarke demonstrated her total ignorance of agriculture by suggesting I drop everything and go and pay Jennifer a visit to put her mind at rest.

"I've actually called to see your husband, Mrs. Mitf

[1]*Locked in jail*

ord…."

"Oh do call me Valerie, dear. Valerie and Hugo - you've known us for years."

"Thanks, err… Valerie. I've actually called to see Hugo about the murder."

She choked on her lemonade. I bet that was a word never heard in this house other than on [1]'Dixon of Dock Green' or 'Cluedo' in its entire history.

"I'm sorry. I didn't mean to offend you. Will your hus… Hugo be available any time today?"

Hugo was in his study, leafing through a pile of papers, signing some and discarding others.

"Hello Meg. What a pleasant surprise. I'd rather talk to you any day than wade through this lot."

He rocked back on his swivel chair and waved an impatient, pinkie-ringed hand over his desk top.

"Valerie says I've to call you Hugo but it'll take me a while to get used to it," I said hesitantly.

"My middle name's Peter - lets go with that."

"It's this and Inspector Fernside. He's put Dan Barber in the lock-up. Can you help me get him out? The very fact he might be involved in this is ludicrous."

"As Magistrate I can't be seen to be impeding the due process of law - but I'm sure something can be done."

[1]*A half-hour television drama about the police*

Dan was eventually released under Peter's recognizance and I was left alone to get on with my work.

I bumped into PC Ryder in the butchers one morning and he gave me the encouraging news that [1]'Maigret' had been hauled back to Penrith to face his superiors over his lack of progress in Nethershaw. As he never reappeared I had to conclude the case had gone cold.

It had been a hard slog for me and my laborers at Ghyll Howe, but I

turned a profit once more - perhaps some of Matt's magic with the soil had rubbed off on me.

Once the immediate chores were out of the way, I paid the lads a bonus, gave them a few days off. and telephoned Joe to come over to look Fairview over.

Of my two opened-up guest rooms, one looked like a junk shop and the other something out of Oliver Twist. I fixed up the second one as well as I could, then bought some fresh bedding and a couple of rugs. It wasn't too bad when I'd finished but the drawers still smelled of fifty years of dust.

It was then I learned what a good chap Joseph Graham was. He'd put on jeans and a t-shirt - admittedly both designer - but he'd come in wellies and a waxed jacket.

He gave me a hand shifting some sacks, then fetched a toolbox from the back of his car, stuck his head under the

[1] *Police detective based on the books of Georges Simenon. Used here in sarcasm*

bonnet of my damaged tractor and after a bit of fiddling about, got the engine turning over. He kicked the tire, then yelled over the din:

"It'll work but you need to get these dents bashed out - they'll damage this, but at least it's useable for now."

Next day, I drove us as far as I could, then we slogged the rest of the way up the fell path to Fairview. On the way up, we became engulfed in a low cloud of drizzle. At least Joe would get an accurate impression of his prospective acquisition.

His immediate reaction was amusement.

"Fairview? It looks straight into the side of another fell. You can't see a bloody thing."

"It's even worse when the mist lifts and you can see the sheep."

The door was more decayed than I remembered, and dung pellets from sheep had blown across what was visible of the path.

The inside still smelled of wet soot but the slates were intact so it was otherwise reasonably dry.

That was about the best I could say for it. It was thick with grime and the windows were obscured by spiders' webs. The rag rugs on the floor were filthy and there were rodent footprints across the dust. I have never in my life been squeamish but this place gave me the heeby-jeebies.

Thinking that Joe must have seen enough I turned to leave, but he walked further into the cottage and took in each room in turn. I'd no idea what he was looking for, but he must have found it because he came out smiling.

"Let's go to the pub."

Chapter Fourteen

The Deal

"I'll give you your asking price plus ten per cent for any extras."

Was he insane? The next gale would blow it flat. Damn - a sheep bumping into it would do the same. What I was thinking must have been written all over my face because he grinned. He took a deep swallow of his beer.

"How much do you want, by the way?"

What to ask? There was no electric or plumbing - the [1]nettie was a shed outside, the only heating was in the kitchen and the water was in a well in the yard. It would need repointing, whitewashing, and imminently a new roof. It no longer had stock or grazing. I should be paying *him*!

"How does five hundred quid sound - plus ten per cent for extras - furniture, outhouse et cetera, which amounts to five hundred and fifty?" he suggested before I could reply.

"It sounds like daylight robbery. I'll take two-twenty."

"Five fifty it is then. It's a generous offer but not out of the way."

"Bloody right it is - it's theft!"

"This has to take the cake as the oddest business deal I've ever done. Usually I'm trying to whittle the price down, not up."

"You must have a plan in mind for Fairview. There's no

[1]*toilet, lavatory*

land attached unless you lease it. I sold it off to buy Ghyll Howe."

"Nope - don't need it. I intend refurbishing it and letting it out. You must have noticed how many fell-walkers there are recently - the numbers increase year by year. I may look to expand around Nethershaw if this goes well. As market towns go it's an attractive place - it has lots of pubs, a bank and food shops. But there are other areas as well; Kendal, Coniston, Ambleside perhaps."

He became lost in thought, working through the problems of converting

a pile of rubble into a desirable holiday let.

"Leave it with me," he said.

The following day he went home. I was sorry to see him go but by midday when I was out sorting the new crop, a Land Rover drew into the yard and out jumped a large man with muscles, who turned out to be the farm manager from Bythwaite.

"Mr. Joseph says you could use a hand sorting staff. What can I do?"

Within the week he'd reduced Dan to the ranks again, hired a professional manager called Dermot O'Connor and instructed me to build him a house. Dermot was tough and straight-forward, and within the month had paid off the workers I had and employed replacements. I'd never realized before just how badly I'd been struggling.

Witch Stones

Over my bedtime [1]Ovaltine one evening, it occurred to me I'd have time on my hands if I could trust this new manager.

I was becoming a gentleman - well, gentlewoman - farmer.

---

[1]*hot malted milk drink*

Chapter Fifteen

A Half-hearted Search for Ellen

One early February day, when the land was still iron-hard and unworkable, I took a trip over to Bythwaite to see Joe. Unfortunately, my Uncle Dick was there. He glowered at me and left the room.

My cousin was left chatting to a young man, who smiled engagingly and offered me his seat beside the fire.

"Meg. This is my good friend Guy Greenwood. He's considering joining my holiday home venture. Guy, Meg is my cousin and owns Fairview which I'm about to buy."

This was far from the truth. Dad had left no Will so I'd have at least to check with Ellen and Johnny. The first loathed the place and the second might be 'in some corner of a foreign field which is forever Johnny Graham' for all I knew. I'd have to suss out Ellen at least and at worst buy her out.

Guy was tall, lean and muscular, his expression serious.

"We've agreed a tentative price of five-fifty for the Fairview property," explained Joe. "It's good I think. Can you stay tonight? If Meg's free we can run over and take a look tomorrow."

I called Dermot and told him I'd some property to vet and would be back the next day.

"Jest as well! That fuckin' bonehead of a lad has gone and put a hammer through the tractor bodywork. Then he dropped the shittin' thing inside the engine!"

"Oh… oh, well - I dare say you'll cope." I said smiling brightly.

Guy had yet to speak. As he didn't look stupid, I took him for the strong silent type.

"Guy's father, Josh Greenwood, is a stakeholder at our largest tenant farm," Joe explained.

"Joe and I have known each other a fair while."

So he did speak - occasionally.

"Try all our lives - well, all mine anyway. He's an old man!" hooted Joe.

I couldn't see much difference between them.

"Four years," said Guy laconically, raising an eyebrow.

"You can run Guy over to Fairview anytime you like, I said to Joe, "but you know my situation with visitors. Better ring the 'Bull' for rooms."

That evening I had a call from Dermot saying the bloody engine had packed in again on the damaged tractor and could he call a mechanic.

I told him fine, and I'd be back the following morning.

"I'll have to take a rain check, I'm afraid," I told Joe ruefully. "There's a matter at Ghyll Howe requiring my checkbook then I've to go to Kendal on an errand."

"We'll meet up in a few days then," said Joe, kissing my cheek.

The tractor problem turned out to be a storm in a teacup. The mechanic had it fixed in no time and left, check in his pocket. If I wanted more freedom, I'd have to start leaving my manager some expenses.

I spent a quiet evening going over work schedules with Dermot then set off early the next morning for Kendal.

The 'private matter' was attempting to locate Ellen so I could sign over Fairview to Joe and Guy. I dropped in at the local cop shop and asked if they knew the whereabouts of Mr. and Mrs. Jonathan Mackie.

"Jonathan Mackie lives over at Ainswick on the Kirkby road but I didn't know there was a Mrs. Jonathan," said the desk sergeant, scratching his head.

Ainswick village was an enormous house with some neat cottages which had once been tithe properties. The house itself was large enough to have a gate-keeper who would have been better suited guarding Wakefield Jail.

"I'd like to see Mrs. Ellen Mackie please. I'm her sister."

"No-one here of that name, but her ladyship might know better. I'll ask Madame if she's at home to visitors."

Damn, and here's me thinking there'd been no royalty in Kendal since [1]Katharine Parr.

"It's urgent I speak to my sister on a legal matter."

He disappeared into the lodge - I assumed to use the

[1]*Sixth and last wife of Henry VIII was from Kendal*

phone - and came back a few minutes later.

"Mrs. Mackie's busy just now but says your sister and Mr. Jonathan divorced years ago. Last she heard she'd moved to the Bahamas with some gigolo from Leeds."

I tried looking up the Bahaman Embassy and Consulate - presumably in London - with the help of the telephone operator and couldn't find either. In the end, I just gave up. If she was in the Bahamas with some gorgeous bloke it was unlikely she'd be returning to Fairview. I had enough to buy them both out, so decided it wasn't worth my while to carry on looking.

The usual clientele in the Lion in Nethershaw grunted a brief greeting and returned to their beers. Dan was in there with 't'wife'. They both smiled, so I guessed Dermot hadn't docked his pay when he was demoted.

Next to a roaring fire which struck sparks from the polished irons on the hearth, sat Mr. Mitford-Clarke and the Methodist minister, Tim Robertshaw, both rosy from the heat. They'd their heads together deep in conversation.

They looked up as I passed and Tim said:

"Hello Meg. Come and sit down - I'll get you a drink."

He rejoined us, my drink in his hand, beaming his perennial smile.

"Hello Peter." I said and noticed Tim's quickly hidden surprise at the familiarity. "How's Valerie?"

"Very well - she'll be pleased to hear about you. We haven't seen you for a while."

"I've been catching up with relatives in Beckton. One of them is interested in buying Fairview. Other than that, training new staff and getting ready for the season's planting."

"And will it be your Uncle Richard who'll be doing the buying?" asked Peter. "He lives over that way, doesn't he? I don't know him myself. He's an acquaintance of Val's"

"He does, but no… my cousin Joseph's the entrepreneur."

There was a protracted pause and I was left with the impression I'd interrupted their tête à tête. Feeling decidedly uneasy I finished my drink and left. They'd resumed their discussion before I was out of the door.

Chapter Sixteen

Guy and the Surprised Reaction

Joe's foreman had hired a firm of builders for Dermot's new house. In all decency I couldn't shift Dan and t'wife from their cottage.

His new home's construction had been left to Dermot to organize. He'd been sharing John-Claude's room in Dan's cottage. If I was in his place, I'd have been laying the foundations myself just to get out.

Clearly Dermot had had the same thought. When I drove into the yard that evening, I found him sorting bricks into a wheelbarrow and trundling it over to the building site. He was whistling and saluted me briefly as he passed.

Joe rang and we made a date to visit Fairview again so Guy could look the place over. I could see the deal going down the drain. My cousin was being overly indulgent, but I couldn't expect his friend to be the same.

After I'd struggled up the stoney path with Joe and Guy, it was with trepidation that I turned the key in the rusty lock. The door creaked on its hinges as I pushed it open.

I'd shown my cousin around without much interest before mention was made of him buying. Now I noticed every minute detail of decay, starting with the door which had rotted away at the bottom. When we entered, I ushered them in, and for a moment or two stood with my eyes shut, before taking in what a shambles it really was. I noticed the mattresses on the beds had rotted, and the old-fashioned bed-steads corroded.

I left them to look the house over, and sat on the wall round the well, ashamed. That day had absolutely nothing going for it. There was a wild wind blowing in from the moors bringing with it needles of sleety rain. Depressed, I pulled my collar up around my ears and waited.

Joe and Guy came out grubbier than they went in but grinning ear to ear.

"First rate!" enthused Guy. "Absolutely perfect. Count me in, Joe."

WHAT?

Joe grabbed me by the arm and dragged me inside. Guy followed us and began to explain:

"We'll turn one of the bedrooms into a bathroom and make the living room and kitchen open plan. The structure needs attention but it's sound. We'll rip off what's left of the plaster, re-do it and leave some natural stone. After that, the biggest job will be replacing windows and doors."

Guy was thinking out loud and was the most animated I'd ever seen him. He pulled me to the window next to the kitchen dresser.

"We'll turn this into French doors opening onto a patio. It has the only good view - not brilliant, but it'd be pleasant on a fine sunny day sitting with an iced drink, gazing down the [1]beck. City people like moors anyway."

"It'll need a new roof as well," added Joe.

"You two are absolutely bloody insane. You're paying me five-fifty. It'll cost the same to renovate it."

[1]stream

Witch Stones

"We could practically rebuild it for that," agreed Guy.

"I hate to burst your bubble but that's precisely what you'll be doing!"

"We'd only need to let it six months of the year for the first two years," Joe enthused. He was getting quite excited. "After that we'll start looking around for something else to invest in."

I was beyond lucky to find the two people on earth daft enough to give me five hundred and fifty pounds for a pile of rubble and still look like eight-year-olds with a box of Meccano.

We went back to Ghyll Howe and at my insistence, went through the figures again. They were right - with careful management there was money to be made.

Guy and Joe departed for Beckton full of ideas for drawing up plans. I

was left with accounts - *again*. Dermot had pretty much everything else under control and his own house was looking good. Bit bigger than I'd intended but he freed me up on the farm so I was inclined to be generous.

My first two years had produced bumper crops - The weather was perfect, the soil rich and productive - even the weevils behaved themselves.

I increased Ghyll Howes' acreage and began saving for extra equipment to diversify swede sold for winter feed and brassica - mostly sprouts and cabbage.

Meanwhile my cousin's hare-brained cottage scheme had turned out to be a real winner. Guy took me up to see Fairview when it was finished. It was gorgeous and I wondered aloud why they didn't just sell it, it'd make a huge profit.

"Who the hell would choose to live up here?" said Guy which surprised me given his previous enthusiasm. "Good holiday home for fell-walkers though."

Once Fairview was complete and let, Joe and Guy bought another derelict cottage not far from Coniston. It looked more like the winter shelter of a shepherd to me, but they'd already proved I didn't understand the property market.

Everything was buzzing along very nicely for the Graham family.

One afternoon as I completed the wages and was putting my books away in the kitchen drawer there was a frenzied thumping on the door.

I ran to open it thinking one of the lads may have been caught in the harvester, but it was Valerie Mitford-Clarke. Her hair on end and her eyes like organ stops, she looked almost wild.

"Meg… Meg, come quick. They've arrested Peter."

She was on the point of collapse so I dragged her inside and sat her at the table.

"Calm down and start at the beginning,"

"I'd just got back from the WI - Mrs. Wilson has taken up macramé, did you know? Her work is extraordinary. You should take a look….." I shook her by the arm.

"Valerie. Peter? Arrest?"

"Ah, yes. Thank you, dear. As I was saying… Bob Ryder has arrested him - he put him in handcuffs and drove him to Penrith," she burst into tears. "They've taken Tim too."

"Why? What did they do?"

"I don't know but Tim was cuffed as well - he was in Bob's car when he came to pick Peter up. "

"Peter's the very definition of respectability so it can't be serious. Do you want me to take you to Penrith?"

"Inspector Fernside said he'd ring later. They'd be in the interview room for at least an hour he said, and I'd only get cold so it'd be better if I stayed at home."

When she stopped long enough to draw breath, I cut in:

"So what are you doing here? You need to be at home to answer the phone. Come on. I'll drive you back. We'll see to your motor in the morning."

She jittered and worried all the way to Luneside, and it was only when I got her home and made her a nice cup of tea she calmed down enough to explain.

Chapter Seventeen

Murder Most Foul

I was absolutely astonished to learn Hugo Peter Mitford-Clarke, dignitary of Nethershaw, and Timothy Robertshaw, minister of the Methodist church, had been arrested for the murder of Matthew Elliot. It was like hearing Pollyanna'd been done for soliciting.

When Fernside phoned, it was to inform Mrs. Mitford-Clarke she wouldn't be needed at Penrith. Her husband and Mr. Robertshaw were being remanded overnight. Spiteful bastard, he could at least have let her visit.

"Do I call Jennifer?" fretted Valerie.

"Not a lot of point. It would take her more than two days to get here. Better wait until you find out something definite. It might just be 'a storm in a teacup'. If you had no inkling, no suspicion perhaps it's just Fernside's imagination."

We sat up talking about anything but her husband, her gardener and the minister until three in the morning, in the hopes of being so tired we'd at least get a couple of hours sleep. It worked for me, but as she still looked frightened and distracted the following morning, I guessed she hadn't slept a wink.

Peter and Tim didn't return home the following day either. The police were examining the derelict allotment and picking through the remains of the shed's foundations. Their prisoners had accompanied them and looked on as the water barrel was examined minutely. Finding nothing, they were obliged to pack up and return their prisoners to the Penrith cells.

This all seemed excessive to me. Surely they should have been bailed, pending their trial but it seemed the world was conspiring against them. The police always seemed to have other questions, other investigations to conclude..

It was a futile exercise. As neither the time of death nor dumping of the body were known, it was difficult to pin anything on either man so they were released, and that would have been the end of it if Peter had been able to bear the guilt.

Such was his shame, he confessed all to his wife and subsequently Bob Ryder. Poor 'Bobby' was shaking like a leaf as he read Peter his rights and they drove to collect Tim. Interestingly, it was the Magistrate and not the Man of God who came clean first.

Valerie and I sat in the visitors' gallery at Kendal Crown Court and listened to the evidence being presented. Jenny had travelled from Canada but wasn't with us as she'd to appear as a witness.

The defendants sat in the prosecution box, smart and trim and straight-backed.

The case for the prosecution was as follows:

Peter had caught Matt in the act of raping Jennifer. Tim had been with him as they'd planned a fishing trip to Windermere. Peter had gone to collect his rod and tackle from its place in the garden shed and he'd caught Matt in the act. He had his hand over a terrified Jenny's mouth and he was gasping into her neck, his trousers round his ankles. Peter sent Jenny into the house to take a bath, warning her she must discuss this with no-one, particularly her mother.

In Court, Jenny, who had been glancing at her father throughout, by the end of her testimony was limp with anguish and had to be helped from the stand. Valerie bolted from the visitors' box but I stayed.

The testimony continued and Mr. Robertshaw was called.

His evidence described how, as he arrived at the shed to help Mr. Mitford-Clarke with his fishing equipment, he became aware of the situation, and perceiving a threat both to his friend and his daughter, he hit Mr. Elliot in the face. The force of his attack knocked the victim over, and Elliot struck his head on a vice attached to the shed's work bench, causing fatal injuries to the rear of his head.

Fearing discovery, the defendants rolled the body in an old rug and loaded it into the back of the minister's car, where under pretext of night fishing, they went to a remote area of Windermere to dispose of the body. There, they weighted it with stones and threw it in the lake.

The following day, first making sure the Misses Elliot were occupied at his chapel, Mr. Robertshaw used the key entrusted to him by the old ladies to enter their home, and disguising his handwriting, wrote a brief note which was shown in evidence and which simply read:

Witch Stones

"Got work down south. I'll be back."

Miss Ruth Elliot burst into tears and blew her nose on a lace-trimmed handkerchief.

"But he didn't.... he didn't... and we never asked why," wept Ruth as her sister looked cynically on.

Over that year, Mr. Mitford-Clarke and the minister took covert trips to Windermere to check the body was still in place.

It was from this point onward their alibi began to unravel, thanks to the local Fishing Club which met every month at the Masonic Hall in Nethershaw. It was here they discussed their mutual interests and raised money for the next season's stocking of a nearby river. As keen fishermen both Mr. Robertshaw and Mr. Mitford-Clarke were members of the Club, the latter being the treasurer.

In conversation at one evening's meeting, the subject got round to pike fishing, which one of the members was keen to try. Aware that Windermere was a prime location for pike, he asked Mr. Mitford-Clarke if another colleague, a Mr. Tebbit, was correct in thinking he and the minister frequented a stretch of water on the south shore of the lake. He had seen them once making their way down a small track between the road and the lake edge.

Robertshaw fudged an answer but fearing discovery of their crime by the fishing fraternity, they agreed to move the body to a safer location.

In a telephone conversation with Jennifer in Canada some months before, she had gone into detail with her father on my new ventures and happened to describe the allotment, now empty, and plastic water-butt. It had clamps to hold it shut she'd told him, and water fed off a gutter through a pipe directly into the barrel. It was never opened she said, because there wasn't any need.

In the small hours of the morning, Peter and Tim went over to take a look, and decided the body would fit and the butt would do as a temporary concealment place until they could think of something better.

But events took a hand, and the minister was called away to the Annual Methodist Council meeting held that year in Newcastle. Unable to move the water-butt himself, Mr. Mitford-Clark was obliged to await his return.

"And has Miss Graham been subpoenaed?" asked the judge.

"She has not, Milord."

"Then see to it at once. Court is recessed until two-thirty," and he struck his gavel on the block.

The clerk of the court was outside the gallery door before I could leave.

"This way Miss Graham. The Prosecutor wishes to see you."

I had been hoping to avoid this. My name would be all over the newspapers and Dan Barber's and Tony Scarr's too since they'd helped me shift the barrel. At least that should provide some light relief while the press tried to make head or tail of their testimony.

Mr. and Mrs. Mitford-Clarke had been so good to me and Jen had been a close friend, but it seemed my testimony could only cause them harm.

Valerie stopped me in the corridor on my way to the Court waiting room. She squared her shoulders and looked me straight in the eye:

"You will please tell the truth - the whole truth. I don't expect you to lie on our behalf and neither will Peter."

Jen stood behind her and hid her face on Valerie's shoulder. When she looked up I was shocked by the hatred in her expression.

"We rescued you when you were out on the street and now you're going to put my father in jail. There's something not quite right about you Meg Graham that you would do this."

"Jennifer, you will apologize and never behave like that again. It isn't Meg who's on trial here," her mother said sharply.

My testimony was as brief and concise as I could make it. I gave details of the discovery and the aftermath. The entire time it felt as if the defendants' eyes were boring into my skull.

Giving evidence is a complex business - I wondered how most people managed it. My concentration was repeatedly broken by movement and shuffling in the visitors' gallery, scribbling and paper rustling from the press box. A jury member sniffed continually. All the time I was conscious of the presence of the two people, one of whom had always treated me as a daughter, whose fate might very well rest in my hands.

The defense chap did his best but there wasn't a lot he could do. He called the two Misses Elliot, but as they thought more of the minister than their own nephew they didn't further the lawyer's cause.

Of course, they were found guilty... they *were* guilty. The jury took five hours to reach their verdict which was read out the following afternoon. The judge's sentencing speech was long and onerous, but the end result was they got the minimum sentence given the accidental and pro-voked nature of their offence. As they both pled guilty to involuntary manslaughter, they were jailed for five years. One life was ended and two ruined beyond repair.

Chapter Eighteen

The Quiet Man

I chickened out of facing Valerie and Jenny after the trial.

On the way to Ghyll Howe I bought a half bottle of brandy, sat at the kitchen table and drank the whole thing, glass after glass. But it made me maudlin, so I swayed myself to bed.

The following morning was even worse. I had the same weight in my stomach but now a hang-over as well. Dermot said:

"By all the saints, you look fit for a knacker's yard. Ring your cousin."

Despite Joe being at the Coniston property, after looking at my grey face in the bathroom mirror, I decided going to Beckton was the best thing to do.

Before I left the following morning, I got up early and ran the steep track to Fairview, thinking perhaps fresh air and exercise might lift my mood.

Half way there and before the track took a sharp bend to the right, I sat on a tussock of grass and took in the vista before me. The entire panorama was bathed in a golden mist, turning the fields to green velvet and glinting off the ribbon of river in the far distance. The town was reduced to a few miniscule grey blocks tossed haphazardly as if by a child's hand. How small it all seemed, dwarfed by the majesty of ancient fells. The arc of cloudless blue sky and the valley beneath put my place in the scheme of things back in proportion.

I continued up the rest of the track, wiping the perspiration from my face with my t-shirt sleeve.

As my childhood home came into view, it became apparent Joe's gamble had been right. Sitting outside were a young couple relaxing in the sunshine. Not wishing to disturb their peace, I skirted the house from the far side of the beck.

Further up the slope I sat again, cogitating on the strangeness of life. I'd grown up here yet it was as if my childhood had never been. I felt no affinity for Fairview. It was as if my life began at the allotment. After that, things had gone so well so when I moved to Ghyll Howe I never gave this place a second thought.

In Beckton, Mrs. Mattison was good enough to provide me with a room despite having no forewarning. I made my way across the road to the pub and was a little surprised in Joe's absence to find Guy there. He smiled a hello and brought me a drink from the bar.

"I understood you were with Joe in Coniston," I said to him.

"I wasn't needed. Joe was seeing the chap from the electricity company to link the cottage up to the grid. Back tonight, I think. The infrastructure's finished but there are the utilities to connect, then plastering and decorating. It should be up and running by the end of next month."

He suddenly realized his mouth was running away with him and blushed.

"Sorry…" he said, embarrassed.

"What on earth for? I've had a shit few weeks. Your enthusiasm is a relief."

My attention had been so taken up with getting to know my cousin, Guy's gentle manner had gone unnoticed.

"Tell me more about the Coniston project. I've been so distracted lately, Joe may have told me things which have gone completely over my head."

"That was pretty much it really. Can I get you another drink?" he said, then reddened again when he noticed my glass was still two-thirds full.

An acquaintance of Guy's came into the bar. He looked so relieved I'd to hide a smile. I was introduced, but then was more than happy to fade into the background as they chatted about local news.

Within the hour, Joe arrived.

"Evening Mr. Graham," said the acquaintance on his way out.

Joe hugged and kissed me then said:

"Ever thought of growing your hair? You look like Peter Pan."

"She does not!" said Guy, on my behalf.

"I do." I said. "Mrs. Mitford-Clarke had it cut off when I had nits."

All the trauma I'd been holding in since the beginning of the trial suddenly broke loose, and I covered my face with my hands and wept.

"I've put in jail the only true father I ever had. I'm a monster!"

Once I began to talk about the trial there was no stopping me. When I'd finished there was deathly silence and I realized the entire bar had been party to my confession.

"Oh, God!" I said.

"Yes, indeed," agreed my cousin, becoming aware of our wider audience:

"Let's get back to the farm so you can meet my mother. She'll like that - she gets little enough company."

At Bythwaite the three of us passed Uncle Dick in the hall as we were coming in and he was going out, leaving a trail of muddy boot prints behind him.

"Sarah!" he yelled, "Look at the mess you've left on this floor - clean it up now."

Joe had hold of my elbow and I felt him stiffen. He had been holding in his resentment his entire life, and for his own part I'm sure he would have left years ago, but his mother needed his care so he felt obliged to stay. I had the impression this venture with Guy was an effort to gain at least some measure of independence.

I'd yet to meet Claire Graham; if at all possible I'd to see if there was anything I could do. Perhaps if she was well enough, she could come to Ghyll Howe from time to time to give Joe a break from his responsibility of care.

When the two men began to discuss electric grids and septic tanks, I wandered over to the window. The sheep on a gentle slope beyond the drystone wall bordering the lawn were nicely fat and had first-class fleeces. They'd make Uncle Dick a tidy [1]bob or two.

There was a quiet bump and a clink of crockery.

"Oh shit!" exclaimed a flustered voice from the hall.

Sarah entered, her plait periodically dunking in the milk jug as she walked. She doled out Swiss-roll with steaming cups of tea. Joe stopped in mid-sentence and glared.

"Take the poker out of your arse," I said once Sarah had left, which made Joe chuckle.

[1]*bring a good price*

Chapter Nineteen
Grace Kelly's Look-alike

Joe excused us to Guy and took me to meet his mother who rarely left her room. I don't know what I was expecting but it certainly wasn't the lady I shook hands with. To describe her wasn't difficult. She looked like a mature Grace Kelly, with hair like spun silk and soft blue eyes.

"I'm very pleased to meet you at last, Aunt Claire - may I call you Aunt Claire?"

"You may not, dear - you will call me Claire." she said firmly and quite lucidly.

"Come and sit down. Go away Joseph," she ordered. He kissed her proffered cheek, grinned at me and left.

Claire studied my face carefully.

"Robert's child, are you? You have a look of him. Very little resemblance to your mother though."

"You knew my mother? I never did - she died just after my brother John was born. I'd be two or three."

She gave a girlish laugh.

"I certainly did, Moira was my sister."

I hadn't known that.

"I'd be interested to learn more about my mother if you don't mind telling me."

Claire walked across the room and opened the top drawer of a sideboard. After carefully sorting through its contents she fetched a photograph for me to see. It was one of those formal studio portraits on stiff card, black and white and a little faded. It showed three children, two girls and a smaller boy.

"That's me," she said, pointing a slender finger at the taller of the girls. "I so hated ringlets - my mother used to wrap our wet hair in rags - it was painful. I remember that dress, it was pale blue organza. I loved it."

She had slipped back into memories of long ago, a faraway look on her face. With an effort, she continued:

"That's your mother, Moira. See how pretty she was? So petite and such lovely dimples, and that's our little brother William. He died not long after this picture was taken - knocked down by a tram on King Street."

Claire turned over the photograph. On the back in faded blue ink was written

Claire, Moira and Willie - 'Forget-me-Not'

"My mother called our house 'Forget-me-not Cottage' even though it was in a suburb of Manchester and had nothing of forget-me-nots or cottages about it. She was very romantic. I'll tell you more about her but not now."

In the blink of an eye, her expression changed and she turned to look tearfully out of the window at a small walled garden, brilliant with multi-hued crocuses.

"Did no-one ever tell you about your mother? How odd," she continued.

I didn't tell her that until I met Joe I didn't even know *she* existed, and he only mentioned her in passing. It's as if she was Mrs. Rochester except she was in a pretty little room full of deep-upholstered furniture and Spring sunshine, rather than a dismal attic. And her companion was a gormless girl called Sarah instead of the dour Grace Poole.

So suddenly it made me jump, she turned and faced me, her eyes wide in horror:

"Don't let him in… please, please don't let him in."

She collapsed hunched on her knees on the floor, staring in panic at the door.

I went to hold her but with amazing strength she pushed me away hard enough to land me on my backside.

I tried again and this time she collapsed against me sobbing in terror.

"Please don't let him hurt me…"

"Who?"

All of a sudden the light returned to her eyes and she sat back on her chair again, gazing into the garden.

"Can I fetch you something? Would you like me to get Joseph?"

Her shoulders slumped.

"No. Nothing but thank you."

I got Sarah to take Claire some tea and went to find Joe. He was talking with Guy in the sitting room and I asked if I could speak to him privately.

"Your mother was unwell just now."

"Did she hurt you? What did she do? I'm so sorry."

He seemed truly worried and I wondered if she really had been responsible for harming someone.

"No she didn't hurt me - she's not big enough, although I must admit I did land on my bum at one point."

"I told you she suffers from dementia. I should never have left you alone with her. She just seemed to be in one of her calmer moods."

This was annoying.

"Joe - I heft sacks of potatoes around and drive a tractor. I'm hardly likely to be fazed by a frail old lady."

He pulled out one of the polished chairs, sat down and buried his head in his hands.

"I don't know what to do, Meg. I've spent my life trying to keep the peace between my parents. For some reason, she cowers in terror every time she sees him, even if she hears his voice."

"Has she seen a doctor?"

"Dad won't allow it. Come on. Guy's waiting."

And just like that he pulled the curtain down on the conversation.

Joe left me in Guy's care and went back to check on his mother. By his demeanor I gathered these outbursts were not uncommon.

It didn't appear to me she had dementia. Her memory didn't seem to be at fault at all - she just seemed terrified. Perhaps a few days away at Ghyll Howe would do her good if Uncle Dick would allow it. She might enjoy a picnic by the river and seeing new faces.

My life had been so full of sadness recently, what with renewed discussion of Matt's death, the trial, the damage caused to the Mitford-Clarkes and now my poor Aunt Claire.

On the pretext of using the bathroom, I slid out of the house and sat in my car to weep.

That's how Guy found me. He knew the gist of my problems but not the details, and just held my hand for a few moments without speaking. Then:

"You're a brave lady. Why don't you stay over and we'll walk the fells towards Scarsdale tomorrow. There's a stone circle up there called the Seven Sisters you might enjoy. It has some local legends attached to it. Joe is at the auction mart with his father tomorrow, so I'm at a loose end. You'd be doing me a favor."

He could of course have gone home, but I appreciated the kindness of his gesture.

Chapter Twenty

The Seven Sisters

Joe and Uncle Dick had taken some of last season's lambs to be sold and didn't expect to be back until late or as Sarah put it:

"They've buggered off to Kendal for t'duration."

I called in on my aunt before Guy and I left for our walk. She was sitting in her chair, gazing absently out of the window. Would it be presumptuous to kiss her cheek, I wondered? I did and she smiled up at me lovingly.

"Hello, dear. You do have something of Moira about you this morning. I love your hair short - it's very becoming. Makes you look like Peter Pan - almost as if you could fly."

I didn't mention the nits.

I didn't think it wise to mention Uncle Dick either, so I said:

"Joseph's taken some lambs to auction, so Guy Greenwood and I are taking a walk to see the 'Seven Sisters.'"

"I'm so pleased, dear. Guy is a sweet boy but shy. He probably needs the walk to the Sisters more than you do. Do you intend visiting Scarsdale? Oh no, how silly of me. You said you'd be walking. That'd be much too far. The Sisters, you say? I know some lovely tales about them. Off you go now," she said, proffering her cheek for a return kiss.

Witch Stones

Guy and I crossed a stile over the lane from the farm gate. It led up a steep incline across other drystone enclosures, dotted with hog-holes in the walls to allow lambs to pass freely from field to field.

We stopped to catch our breath at the top and looked down on Bythwaite below. To one side was a small wood, and beyond the farm buildings an expanse of green pasture.

"Do you know what Bythwaite means?" Guy asked absently. I shook my head.

"Its old Norse dialect for 'Bee Meadow'. Many of the old farmers - my own father included - still speak it fluently."

"That's lovely. It smacks of beehives and honey and sweet golden things,"

Guy grinned.

"For a spud farmer, you've a rare poetic turn of phrase."

We rounded a rocky outcrop and the Sisters were before us - close enough to touch, upright fingers of limestone studded with prehistoric crustacea and set in a perfect circle. Mossy and weathered, the largest stood nearly seven feet tall.

I gazed at them silently. There was absolutely no doubt at all that this was a sacred place. It had a murmuring presence, almost as if the stones sang. Why they sang was another matter. As if he'd heard my thoughts, Guy said:

"The old folks have many stories about them but all I remember hearing is that they represent seven mothers. A fertility cult perhaps? I don't know.

"There's another, bigger circle further down the hillside, but it's frequently visited by tourists and it's always seemed to me the spirits of the place fled long ago.

"Scarsdale is over the brow of the hill. We can look if you like. On foot it's a difficult walk over scree on a steep slope so I'll drive you there sometime if you wish."

The hill above Scarsdale Manor Farm steepened sharply the few yards to the top. It had been worth the short climb. Spread below was a little Shangri La enclosed by steep fells. A complex of barns with a large house stood below. It was hemmed in by a patchwork of fields, some the pale gold of growing wheat, others with the softness of flower-studded grass. They were bisected by a river and I could make out a small bridge through the trees which lined its banks.

"It's beautiful except in the winter. The hills mean we get more than our fair share of snow and most years we are locked in. We can batten down and that's fine, but problems arise if a doctor's needed.

"Our housekeeper's pretty good though. Her mother trained her in the old medicine - she has a cupboard full of herbs - and I've known her take out an appendix before now."

He looked grim for a moment, then smiled

"The patient survived and stands before you."

Chapter Twenty-one

Dick, Deidra and Dermot

When we returned to Bythwaite, my uncle was back from Kendal and sitting grim-faced in the sitting room wearing work overalls which seemed to be his only mode of dress. Joe was in the act of dropping ice into a couple of glasses of Scotch and had [1]a face like a fiddle.

"Want one?" he asked Guy and I without his usual warmth, the inference being we might need it.

We sat round sipping in silence waiting for Uncle Dick to have his say.

"Th'art Robert Graham's daughter from Nethershaw?"

"I am."

"And - Robert Graham's daughter - [2]what a'rt doing in my house and whats t'a want?"

"Joseph bought my house for his new business, and if it wasn't for the affection I bear him and your wife, I'd be down the road on my way home.

There was a deathly hush, and I took in the reaction of each person in the room.

Joseph looked frozen in shock; Guy had moved to stand at my shoulder while Uncle Dick sipped his whisky smiling wryly. Joe's reaction pretty much became my own.

"Moira's blood - not your father's I see."

Now what the hell did *that* mean?

[1]*a sour expression*
[2]*What are you doing in my house and what do you want*

"I've no intention of welcoming you to Bythwaite - there are matters tha knows [1]nowt about and nor shall learn from me. But you may visit Joseph and Claire if tha lets me know when. [2]I'll tek misen off."

"I'm more than happy to do as you ask - I have no more wish to spend time with you than you apparently have with me.

"I'll [1]*tek misen off* to my own farm. My manager will be requiring my assistance by now. Goodbye sir, I will ring before my next visit," I declared sarcastically.

I was gratified to see the look of surprise on his face when I mentioned my farm, and that I had a manager. I grinned at Joe behind my uncle's back as I closed the door.

Dermot's house was finished and I was very much surprised to find a Mrs. Dermot installed. She was standing with both feet on a fork trying to unearth clumps of grass to make a garden. She'd managed one corner but there was an awful lot yet to go.

As I pulled up before my house door, Dermot yelled over his shoulder:

"Deidra, come and meet the Boss."

She wiped the perspiration and the soil from her hands with her pinny, and rather than walk to the gate vaulted over the low fence.

Deidra O'Connor was definitely an Irish lass although her

[1]*nothing*
[2]*arrange to be elsewhere*

accent had become confused with the brogue of Nether-shaw.

She was wiry and strong.

"And a good mornin' it is, Ma'am," she said when Dermot introduced her. Then she turned and yelled behind her:

"Get yer arses out here yer little buggers and meet the lady whose payin' fer yer keep."

There were only three children, but then I hadn't known there were any, or a Mrs. Dermot either come to that.

The O'Connor boys were polar opposites to the Barber kids. Neat and clean, all three boys politely shook my hand and said:

"Pleased to meet you, Miss Graham."

There were twins, Sean and Paul aged ten and little Robin, five and in his first year of primary school. They all had their mother's freckles.

Dermot straightened up and said proudly:

"Sean here wants to go back to Ireland and fight the IRA - he ruffled his son's hair proudly and Sean smiled up at him. Paul wants to be a doctor. He'll make it - he's streets ahead of any doctor I ever met, and Robbie has in mind to be Flash Gordon from the comic books."

"No farmers then?"

"Not bloody likely," said their mother. "Dermot already carts half of Westmoreland into the house on his boots. I don't want the other half as well."

Witch Stones

I was getting to like this woman. She called it as she saw it. I was looking forward to introducing her to Uncle Dick.

"Skidaddle!" said Dermot, clapping his hands. The boys ran back inside and Deidra returned to her gardening.

"There's a question I have for you Miss Graham," said Dermot. "The lads are due to start school in Nethershaw after Easter. Will you take them to meet the school master? It's more than my life's worth to let Deidra loose on a man o' learnin'"

"I wouldn't worry about that. Mr. Richardson and his sister are Nethershaw born and bred - he's heard it all."

Dermot still looked doubtful.

"I'll go with her if you like, but she really does need to meet the locals. You're not Catholic?" I asked as an afterthought.

"Did yer not comprehend what I said about Sean defendin' the Union?"

"Then you'll not have a problem," I said, accidentally adopting his accent. "Like most country towns in this part of the world, the townsfolk are either Methodist or [2]C of E. and they fight over *that*."

"That'll please the wife. She's not averse to a bit of 'We plough the fields and scatter' of a Sunday morning and if there's a [1]WI she'll be made up."

[1]*Women's Institute. A Christian organization run by women for women*
[2]*C of E - Church of England*

"Definitely a WI," I said with a laugh, imagining Deidra taking tea with the Misses Elliot.

After what had happened to their nephew, I wondered if the ladies would take exception to me attending the morning service. I would be interested to see what they'd done about the minister. Valerie and Jen were [2]C of E so I wouldn't bump into them. I wasn't ready for that and I shouldn't think they were either.

Dermot went about his work and I entered the kitchen to find an Irish stew, a bowl of mashed swede and cabbage and a half pint of beer on the table.

I was so hungry it didn't touch the sides.

When I'd finished, Deidra appeared as if by magic to clear the pots and asked:

"What will be yer delight for tomorrow, Miss? A pork chop or a nice fat trout from the river?"

"I'm very grateful to you Deirdra, but there really is no need."

"No trouble at all Ma'am. Think of it as part of my man's wages - I'll bill you the cost of the food but the labor's my pleasure..... at least it is until those bastard kids muck up a good thing and you won't let us through the front door."

For the life of me, I couldn't believe that day would ever come.

It was time to turn out the farm's bedrooms and see to their decoration and furnishing. I loaded the tractor with the old crap I'd rooted out and drove it myself to the village hall for the next jumble sale. After, I picked up my car and drove to Kendal, furniture shopping.

Everything I did now put me in mind of that grim homestead on the moors, having money to spend most of all.

'Baker and Stoddart', the furniture shop in Kendal, undertook to deliver everything within the week and said their chaps would lay the carpets and carry the furniture upstairs for me. I smiled inwardly. They hadn't seen how narrow and steep the stairs were yet.

I accompanied Deidra to the chapel the following day. She'd scrubbed the kids clean until their faces were raw but could do nothing about the skinned knees, showing below their short trousers.

The Misses Elliot saw my hesitation and greeted me like a long lost friend. I hoped I could be as generous of spirit if somebody stuffed Johnny into a water barrel.

I introduced them to Deidra, hoping against hope she'd been taught not to take the Lord's name in vain in his own house.

Surprisingly, her Irish accent virtually disappeared. Even her boys looked amazed.

"Good day to you, ladies. Delighted to make your acquaintance. These here are my lads, big ones're Sean and Paul, little 'un's Robbie. I'll be wanting to register them with the Sunday School."

Sean and Paul's shoulders slumped. There's nothing worse for a boy's prestige with new kids than being seen leaving Sunday School. The Misses Elliot of course ran the Sunday school.

"Do they play games?" asked little Robbie hopefully.

The replacement minister was clearly a fill-in. He was small and thin and his sermon was based on the sin of adultery - not a wise subject in a small country town where it was the major pastime. Still he managed to mumble his way through all the shifting and tittering from the boys in the back pews.

On the steps afterwards, Deidra was formally adopted by the ladies of the WI, and Mrs. Wilson showed her the macramé handbag she'd just completed.

She was also introduced to Mr. Richardson, the Headmaster and I winced when she greeted him with:

[1]"A lick of t'stick's what they need from time to time. Don't trouble 'bout laying it on thick."

As they'd been whisked off to the Sunday School by Marjorie Elliot, her lads were spared even more embarrassment.

It being Nethershaw, the Methodist chapel where everyone had [2]signed 'the Pledge', had emptied into the various pubs around town. There, they got to the bars quick before

't'other lot' whose service ended half an hour later, could

[1]*A dose of the cane is what they need from time to time. Don't worry about giving them a good whack.*
[2]*Strict Methodists are required to sign an undertaking to abstain from alcohol called The Pledge*

beat them to it.

I found Dermot, deposited his wife with him, and left the boys on a bench outside with other like children, including Dan Barber's little horrors. Then I [1]scarpered sharpish in case the Mitford-Clarkes made an appearance.

[1] *left quickly*

Chapter Twenty-two

Gift and a Home in the Making

I arrived back at Ghyll Howe to find Guy and a couple of men I took for his farmhands, standing in the yard distracting my staff from their work.

It turned out he'd brought us a load of sheep manure from Scarsdale. He'd arrived with it in a truck dripping excrement all over my clean arable yard. Still it was free and the best fertilizer there was. If he thought I'd be impressed by half a ton of sheep shit he was…. absolutely right. It should increase my carrot yield by half.

Avoiding liquid poo in pale green kitten heels fit only for chapel is not an easy task but I managed it without too much damage.

Guy turned when he heard me cursing and his eyes nearly popped out of his head. What was he staring at?

"You look… nice," he stuttered. All my men - and his - were trying to suppress grins. I waved them off.

"Just back from chapel."

"You can't be walking in slurry in those shoes," he said lifting me in his arms and carrying me into the house. I had never been coddled in my entire life. In fact, I was more used to driving the harvester and swearing like a trooper when it got stuck.

Guy suddenly realized he might have overstepped the mark and almost dropped me in mortification.

"Tea?" I asked, that being my automatic response to any sticky situation.

After clearing his throat, Guy said he realized I was busy but if I had an hour or two spare would I like to visit Kendal? He'd this load to drop off for me then go on to pick up some things his father needed on the farm.

I'd to plead work - I really didn't have the time, what with organizing the refurbishment of the farmhouse and checking on Dermot's shiny new abode.

"I'll be back over in a few days. I have some questions for Uncle Dick. Perhaps I'll see you then?"

He smiled at the expression on my face. It was going to be dreadful.

If I was paying for Dermot's new house, I should make sure Mrs. O'Connor wasn't decorating the place with chandeliers and Persian carpets, but I needn't have worried:

[1]"Bloody 'ell, yer ladyship," said Deidra, formalities shelved. "You might 'ave given warnin' - now I'll 'ave to shift this broom to melting."

"Well fuck me... so you 'aven't. [2]That one'd passed me by completely. Come on then - get a shift on. I've dinner to put on t' stove."

[1]Bloody hell, your Ladyship. You might have given me warning. Now I'll have to sweep like a maniac
[2]I'd completely forgotten. Come on then - hurry up. I've dinner to cook.

"You'll do no such thing, Deidra. I only want a quick look round. I've not seen the house yet."

Was this the same woman who said 'delighted to meet you' to Ruth and Marjorie Elliot?

She whisked me round the three bedroomed house at a trot. The twins shared a large room but Robbie had the little box-room. Everything was neat, clean and orderly but there was decorating still to do and the little one was sleeping on a mattress on the floor. I'd ring Bakers and ask them to add a single bedstead to my order.

I spent a few days organizing the fertilizing and sowing with Dermot and going over his account books. I'd given him a generous amount of what he labelled 'petty cash' to cover most day to day expenses, which I hoped would release me from more mundane work.

Ghyll Howe Farm's newly refurbished bedrooms made the rest of the house look shabby so I decided it needed a face-lift.

The decorator assisted by his two sons papered the bed rooms I'd done my best with, and I allowed myself a grin as the furniture men puffed, panted and swore their way up the narrow stairs.

Deidra came in as they were doing it, took a good look at the rooms, stole five pounds from Dermot's petty cash tin and made curtains on an ancient treadle sewing-machine - in repayment for Robbie's bed she said, although I knew it was from the goodness of her heart.

Witch Stones

I was about to ring Joe when he bowled into the yard in his Healey with Guy in the passenger seat. The decorators were doing the downstairs and the place was completely up-side-down with dust-sheets everywhere.

We shimmied our way between piled-up tables and chairs and I showed them what I'd done with the two bedrooms.

Joe was surprised at the change - so amazed I really thought he might have been a bit more tactful when he said:

"Good God, Meg! From a pig-pen to a palace - what on earth provoked this?"

"It so happens it was you, you ungrateful sod," I said, and thought of the original reason for the redecorating, my aunt.

Chapter Twenty-three

[1]"Got ter Specerlate t' Acoomerlate"

I decided to trust Joe with my musings.

"While I was talking to your mother, I did wonder if it might help to get her out of the house for a day or two. There are some nice walks hereabouts and we could take a picnic down to the river if the weather cooperates. How many years is it since she left Bythwaite? There's space here now if you'd like to use it."

"I don't think Dad would go for it."

"If it puts his mind at rest you could come too."

"Why don't you come to Beckton for a few days?" said Joe. "That'd give you chance to get your house livable in again and we could tackle Dad together."

"Make it a couple of weeks. I need to get round my customers. They've been shoved to the bottom of my list of priorities and unless I get cracking I'll be bankrupt by the end of the season. I need to employ a salesman; there's no way I can offload that responsibility. In any case your dad might throw me out after our last encounter"

"Why not employ a salesman then?"

He ignored my reference to his dad completely.

"Despite appearances," I glanced back at all the crap overflowing from my house on account of the decorators, and packaging dumped by the furniture fitters,

"I'm not made of money."

[1]*Got to speculate to accumulate*

Witch Stones

Joe looked the other way at orderly fields of sprouting crops in good rich soil under a perfect late spring sky and raised an eyebrow.

"I'd say you'll be doing well again this year. That's four in a row. I never met anyone starting out who got four years of good weather. You should reinvest while the going's good."

A hand shoved him to one side.

"You'll be excusing me gentlemen. I need to speak to the Boss on an urgent matter," said Dermot.

I followed him into his office.

"I've been doing my best to make things work Miss Graham, but there's a limit. I need to take on another six lads - don't need to be skilled labor.

"We've another three acres and we've diversified to other crops which are more labor intensive. It isn't working. Here's the books.

"And we need two more tractors. The old one's held together with spit and chewing gum and the others are looking bloody ropey too. And next year we'll need another harvester."

I must have looked ill because he gave me a considering look and added philosophically:

"Got ter specerlate t' acoomerlate."

I snatched the account and diary ledgers he handed me, muttering that he was so sharp one of these days he'd do himself an injury.

"I'll take them away and give them a good look over. Just do the best you can."

This was unusual coming from Dermot so I followed up with:.

"You didn't by any chance overhear Mr. Graham discussing finances for the next year?"

"Might of," he answered smugly.

"Will you allow me to go through those with you?" asked Joe once Dermot left, then put up defensive hands when I replied:

"You've done enough bloody damage. He caught the gist of new tractors. He'll be like a dog with a bone, dammit."

"He's an employee, for God's sake."

"He's not an employee 'for God's sake' - he's my right-hand man and if you cut my right hand off I'll bleed to death."

It suddenly occurred to me:

"His wife could swear for England but I'd never manage without her either."

More thought:

"And no matter Deidra's opinions on the matter, Dermot's bringing those three lads up to be farmers. But I'd be grateful for your help with the books."

Once Joe and a diffident Guy had left, I spent almost the whole of two weeks trailing round from customer to customer over most of Westmoreland and practically the whole of the West Riding of Yorkshire. It was easier now I was dealing with wholesalers rather than individual out-lets. I could do all the meetings and greetings well, but I'd risen above my ability to generate new business. You can only teach yourself so much and I suppose I still came across as a rough diamond, with callused hands and a broad accent.

Posh chaps from London - for that's what most of the higher-ups were - I found supercilious and objectionable, and I supposed it must have shown. Joe was right. Either I needed a salesman with the right accent or I was stuck.

Did I want to climb higher up the ladder? People born to abject poverty are always insecure, so the answer had to be yes.

Commitments honored, I drove to Bythwaite and despite his father's antipathy, Joe insisted I stay at the farm.

The room I was shown to by Sarah - "call me Connie … you know - like Connie Francis," - was plush, airy and comfortable.

"But your name's Sarah!"

"Well? I can be Connie if I like. Ain't no law agin it." she pouted with an appalling American accent.

Uncle Dick might be seriously rethinking the new TV he'd had installed.

"Mum says to tell thee tea's five sharp. Be there," and with that she skipped off down the landing to a loud ren-dition of 'Who's Sorry Now?'.

Chapter Twenty-four

Dastardly Dick

"You didn't tell me you'd be coming - we agreed," glowered Uncle Dick as we sat round the tea table.

"True, I didn't. If I had you wouldn't have been here and I wanted to speak to you."

"What about?" said Uncle looking defensive.

"Nothing you need worry about. I'm a busy farmer so had given little thought to the house I live in until now, so I've fixed it up. When I met Claire it occurred to me it might be good for her to spend a few days at Ghyll Howe to give her a change of scenery."

"She's too sick," said Uncle Dick shortly.

"Obviously I know she's unwell. I've spent time with her," I said impatiently. "I haven't seen anything I couldn't cope with, and Joe can accompany her if it puts your mind at rest."

"Joe's too busy with his new business and t'farm. He can't come. I said no."

"I could do with a couple of days off," said my cousin.

"You can slope off to Nethershaw? You were too busy to help with the lambing this year - I'd to get Albert Brookbank's lad in. How come you've time to squire your mother around Westmoreland," and turning to me he said:

"And what are you still doing here? Your business with Joseph is finished, so why haven't you taken yourself off?"

"I hardly think a couple of days in Ghyll Howe constitutes 'squiring around Westmoreland'," I muttered.

I could feel my temperature rising which would be disastrous so I excused myself to get some air and walked round the copse beside the house.

"Bastard!" I cursed. "BASTARD!"

"Shut up," hissed Joe between the trees. "He'll hear you."

"He's not bloody-well winning this round. I'll get your mother to Ghyll Howe if I've to kidnap her!"

"That wouldn't be clever. You'll need to charm him."

"What me?" I laughed. "I'm about as charming as Winston Churchill."

Negotiations recommenced over breakfast the following day. My uncle and Joe had been up since daybreak out on the fells, so they were starving when they sat down to eat.

'Connie' plonked bacon, sausage, eggs, mushrooms and a cob of bread on the table and went back for the tea.

"Before you start yer badgerin' my girl, she's not going."

I put on my sweetest smile and said:

"Now Uncle Dick, don't you think a couple of days away would do her good? Why don't you come too? You'd be more than welcome."

Ugh!

My attempt at charm must have been lacking as Joe, napkin covering his mouth, excused himself on the pretext of making a phone call.

Witch Stones

[1]"You've buggered up my appetite with your moithering. I'm off," said my uncle, dropping his knife and fork on his plate with a clatter.

Later, when his father had gone to bed, Joe asked if I'd like to go with Guy and him to Coniston the next day.

"Think I'll keep your mother company for a while. Don't worry I'm not daft enough to tell her what we've been saying."

I spent an hour or two of the afternoon with my aunt. She seemed to like my company and chatted away cheerfully until at one point, on hearing

footsteps in the hall, she looked panic-stricken and grabbed my hand.

But the footsteps passed and so did her mood.

Claire led me through a half-glazed door into her garden. She tended the flowers in her little retreat herself she told me. She snipped a scented rose from a trellis on the house wall, brushed off its thorns with gloved

fingers and folded my hand around its stem.

"For you, Moira dear," she said and kissed my cheek.

I'd little time to wonder about her sad remark, other than to consider if the slip hadn't sunk my plans without trace.

Joe came in before we could say more, full of enthusiasm from his day away. It made her smile.

[1]*You've ruined my appetite with your nagging. I'm leaving*

All the aggravation was now centered on meal times since that was when Uncle Dick and I ran into each other.

Come what may, I'd to return home the next day and I still hadn't solved the problem of my aunt. I was just about to open my mouth and more than likely make matters worse, when Uncle Dick's eyes narrowed and he all but spat at me:

"Keep your fucking mouth shut or I'll shut it for you. She's not going and that's flat."

"There's no need...." began Joe.

"And you'll keep your trap shut too or you'll feel my belt."

This was to a son who was well into adulthood.

There was a short silence while everyone lost their appetites and Uncle Dick tucked into his steak pie.

A soft voice broke the silence.

"I'm sorry to contradict you in front of guests Richard, but I shall be accompanying Meg home for two days at the end of which time, I may or may not return here as I decide."

We all turned round in amazement to see Claire holding herself upright on the doorjamb, her face deathly pale but with her lips pursed in determination.

"Out! OUT!" her husband screamed at her. "You've no say in this, Go to your room!"

"For God's sake Uncle she's a grown woman, not a six year old child. She's allowed to say and do what she wants and 'going to her room' isn't even an option."

"She behaved fine until you showed up. You're like my fucking brother all over again. Pack your bags and never show your face here again."

"Glad to," I grimaced, "but should she want to, Claire is still coming with me. She can stay at Ghyll Howe for as long as she wants."

Joe followed his father's orders and taking his mother by the arm, he walked her back to her room. I was disgusted with his lack of backbone. I expected better of him.

It was only at this point it sank in what Dick had said about my father.

.

Chapter Twenty-five

The Seven Sisters and Joshua Greenwood

An hour later I was still suffering with shock and disappointment that Joe had offered no explanation for his *volte-face* over his mother, so when he returned I continued the conversation my uncle had interrupted.

Within the hour, I was stowing my suitcase on the back seat of my car ready for an early start and Joe was leaning against the bonnet looking thoughtful.

"Joe… about your mother," I began.

Ignoring me completely he said:

"I'll just go ring Guy again. Why don't you drop by Scarsdale in the morning. You'll have plenty of time to get home if you set off early," and without a 'by your leave' he strode back into the house.

In the doorway he bumped, literally, into Sarah 'Francis'.

"Guy's on t'phone. Sez he wants to talk to you Joe. Hurry up."

"Mr. Joseph and Mr. Greenwood," said Joe automatically, pushing past her.

"Well, that's settled then. He'd called to suggest just the same thing. Watch out! Seems to me he's smitten!"

"Thank you. At what point were the two of you going to ask me what I wanted to do? I may have business of my own."

"Do you?" asked Joe, raising his eyebrows.

"Nothing immediate," I conceded irritated, "but it would have been nice to be asked."

"Right you are then. I'll get Sarah to make you some breakfast for seven. I've to visit tenants tomorrow with Dad so we should be gone by six. Give me a ring when you get home.

"It's a direct route to Scarsdale and a bit overgrown but once the road turns sharply upwards you'll know you've passed it. Turning round on the hill's a bugger so be careful - and just pray you don't meet anything coming the other way."

Claire was still asleep when I left so I kissed her cheek and tiptoed to the door. The Lord alone knew when or if I'd ever see her again.

I straightened my back. I *would* see her again, even if I'd to break in in the dead of night.

Finding Scarsdale Manor Farm turned out to be something of a problem. Joe hadn't been wrong about the roadside hedges. They were dense and difficult to see over. I missed the gate of Scarsdale, only realizing my error when the road took a sudden upwards swing towards the ridge hiding the Seven Sisters. It took six gear changes to turn the car around on the narrow lane and bump and jolt back the way I'd come.

Guy met me at a gate half-hidden by a wild rose in full bloom.

Scarsdale was a farm originally attached to a sixteenth century manor house, of which only the overgrown outline remained, except for a low wall which supported a corrugated hut. It had had bits and pieces added to it here and there over the years, and the overall effect was of a peaceful home in a stunning location.

On a small lawn between the storm-porch and beaten earth path was a large rustic table and complementing chairs, where sat a man in his sixties, with collar length white hair, badly cut, and a poorly shaven chin.

He smiled an invitation for me to be seated, and Guy held out a chair.

"Father, this is Margaret Graham, Mr. Robert's daughter. Meg, this is my father Josiah - Josh - Greenwood."

"Is she now!" exclaimed Josiah eyeing me curiously. "Guy speaks well of thee, Miss Graham."

"Please call me Meg Mr. Greenwood. It's a pleasure to know you."

A girl in her early teens arrived carrying a bare wooden tray with mugs of steaming tea and a milk jug. She curtseyed unsteadily. Guy dashed to help her before she dropped the lot, and placed the tray on the table, smiling kindly at the girl as he dismissed her.

He took the chair next to mine and sipped his own tea politely while his father apologized for a 'slurp'.

Searching for something to say, I began:

"Guy was telling me about the Seven Sisters. I understand the land they stand on is yours."

Witch Stones

[1]"Dick Graham's, but I graze a few yaws there from time to time. There's a reet o' way runs across it so it's not much use; f'sheep in any case. 'as other uses I'm told."

"I thought to take Meg a walk round the south meadows, to the mill." said Guy to his father, "Coming?"

I hid my amusement behind my mug - it was apparent from his tone that was the last thing on earth he wanted.

[2]"Nah. You young'uns go enjoy thysel's. I can alus find occupation in t'office," he said gloomily.

Guy and I strolled along a path across an extensive hay meadow. On the far side, a tractor had stopped mowing and the driver had joined half-a-dozen young men scattering the cut grass with forks. The fragrance carried clear across to where we stood. At the bottom of the field, Guy helped me over a stile onto a riverside path, where a row of dead crows and one brightly feathered jay were tied by their legs to the fencing in an ineffective attempt to deter other birds from eating the cereal crops. I shuddered with distaste.

"Next field up's wheat. Doesn't work, but the theory is if your father did it, there must be some merit," said Guy with a shrug.

The river's smooth rocks forced the water into pools and eddies, overhung by willow and elm, but it was easily

[1]*Dick Graham's but I graze a few ewes there from time to time. There's a right of way runs across it so it's not much use. For sheep anyway. It has other uses, I'm told.*
[2]*No, you youngsters go and enjoy yourselves. I can always find things to do in the office.*

crossed. Guy hopped from stone to stone, holding his hand out to help me over.

Once safely across, we followed the river path to an ancient watermill. Guy told me there had been one on that spot for a thousand years. In the old days, all the surrounding smallholdings would bring their corn for grinding.

We wandered back to the farmhouse, crossing a cobbled pack-bridge and passing along a lane hedged with bramble and blackthorn.

It had been a wonderful morning - so badly needed, and such were my feelings of oneness with nature, I was surprised to find I had unwittingly taken Guy's hand. He was looking down at our intertwined fingers in surprise. I pulled away, but he took my hand again and drew it through his arm, saying nothing but walking forward, gazing ahead as if nothing out of the way had happened.

Before I left, I said my goodbyes to Mr. Greenwood.

[1]"Nay, Bob's lass - who'd a thawt it? Come back soon."

I climbed into my car and smiled up at Guy through the open window.

"Thank you so much. I can't remember when I spent such an enjoyable morning. I'm so happy I came."

"It was my pleasure. I wonder if…. no… it doesn't matter. Drive steady," he said and he walked away without another word.

[1]*Unbelieveable. Bob's daughter. Who'd have thought it*

Witch Stones

They were an odd lot round Beckton.

Chapter Twenty-six

Joe's Read the Riot Act and Deidra Saves the Day

I'd left a few items at Bythwaite so I thought to nip in, pick them up and leave again. I'd no time to waste if I was to get home before dark.

I quailed inside at the thought of the unpleasantness to come should my uncle be back. Uncle Dick and I shared bloody-mindedness in spades, or he wouldn't have run a huge farm with tenants, and I wouldn't have hoisted my-self from an orphaned waif to an arable farmer with a steadily accruing bank balance.

We had to find a way to compromise or there was going to be another permanent rift, with my frail aunt caught in the middle.

On the hall table at Bythwaite was an envelope addressed to 'Margaret Graham, Ghyll Howe Farm, Nethershaw'. It had clearly been placed there ready for the post. I opened it.

"Come and take the stupid woman and good rid-dance. If she begs to come back, I'll think on it - no promises, mind. Joe stops here. He has respon-sibilities to this farm and I'll not see him slide his way out of them.

As for you. You have split this family in two. I hope you're pleased with yourself. After what your fa-ther did I could have expected no different. You won't darken this door again in my life-time nor set foot on my land - there'll be no permission granted."

It was signed *'Richard C Graham'*.

Joe came in just as I finished reading, and I thrust the sheet of paper in his hands in exasperation. He read it and flung it in the sitting room fire.

"It's time you stood up to him," I said angrily. "You've to decide which side of the fence you're on. As she's made her wishes clear, your mother's coming to Ghyll Howe - that's no longer up for discussion. Will you be coming too, or as he says in that," I pointed at the note curling to ash in the flames, " fulfilling your obligations to Bythwaite?

"Your choice. I was heading home in any case. I suggest you consider your course of action carefully. Just bear in mind you may be involving Guy and Mr. Greenwood in this as well."

"Dad's too much of a realist to let Josh go. He's the best tenant with the biggest farm on Bythwaite. I'll think on it."

"Get a shift on then - don't dawdle."

The drive back to Nethershaw began slowly, with the winding country lanes. Once I got on the main Kendal road it was much easier and I found myself with time to mull over what my uncle had said.

I had NO idea what my father had done to cause such a savage response. The only possible remaining link after he'd moved to Fairview appeared to be between my mother and her sister, my aunt Claire.

Witch Stones

I began to be concerned the following day when Joe hadn't called as promised. There was no word from him the day after either.

To keep myself occupied, I had some of the lads haul loaded sacks onto a lorry for delivery. Dermot drove and I was pleased to see he'd decided to take his son Sean with him. Better a land-worker than dead on the streets of Belfast.

A further two days after that, just as I was beginning to think Dick had actually taken a cleaver to his wife and son, Joe's Healey turned into Ghyll Howe and mother and son emerged.

My aunt looked on the point of collapse, so between us we got her up the steep stairs to her bedroom and Joe put a match to the fire laid in the grate. I'd done my best with the rooms but they still lacked the comfort of Bythwaite and she'd no garden to potter in. I'd figure something out.

"You look about as [1]chipper yourself," I observed to my cousin. "You're next door. Go and sleep."

"I'll just bring the bags in….."

"You can do that later. If you're worried about being seen without your draws, you can always push the blanket box behind the door."

He smiled and kissed my cheek.

"Thanks, Meg."

[1]*healthy*

When they were both settled, I ran next door to Dermot's in a panic.

"Deidra - Dee-dra! What do I do? I've unexpected guests. I've two who'll expect more than Heinz soup and corned beef sarnies. What do I do?"

Domesticated I wasn't. Give me a field of vegetables to harvest or a hen to pluck and gut I was fine but confront me with a working kitchen and I went to pieces.

Deidra jumped the fence, ran into the yard and dragged me into my kitchen.

"Sit down I'll put t'kettle on."

"What do I do? I wasn't expecting them and I've nothing to feed them with."

"Here, drink your bloody tea," she said shoving the mug in my hand, "then put your brain into gear. You're sitting on God knows how many tons of vegetables and I wrang the neck of a capon this morning. I can soon knock up some rice-pud for afters or there're still some apples from before Christmas in t'loft.."

"What's ta problem? Queen's not coming, is she? She'd have all on getting her carriage up yon lane."

Deidra hadn't spoken like that when I first met her. She'd clearly ditched Ireland for the Lake District.

"Cooker might as well be christened feeding Liz and Phil," she said without the glimmer of a smile. "Here - peel those apples then go next door and set the table for eight."

"Eight?"

"If I'm doing all the fucking work, least you can do is feed my family."

Fair enough.

And that's why, when Joe and Claire came into *my* kitchen it smelled of chicken stew and dumplings, then apple pie with custard.

I introduced a scrubbed and polished Dermot, Deidra and offspring to my aunt and Joe.

"Pleased to meet you," said Dermot politely.

"Hello, Mrs. Graham and Mr. Graham," said the O'Connor twins in unison.

[1]"Put your arse on that chair yer ladyship," said Deidra, treating my kitchen as her own, "and tuck in. Put a bit of color in your cheeks."

There was one of two ways to treat Deidra - either you laughed or cried.

I'm delighted to say Joe and Claire laughed, and by the end of the meal my aunt was indeed rosy cheeked and Joe had relaxed, stuffed full.

[1]*Sit on that chair your ladyship and eat*

Chapter Twenty-seven

The Beginnings of a Business Plan

After the meal was complete, and Claire and Joe were seated in the living room chatting with Dermot, Deidra dumped the pots in the sink and threw me the tea towel.

We worked for some time in silence then:

"Thank you Deidra. That was kind of you."

"Not used to folks diggin' you out of the shit then, Maggie?"

Maggie? I hadn't been Maggie since Mrs. Mitford-Clarke renamed me at Luneside House.

I wasn't aware my aunt had entered the kitchen until:

"You come in t'kitchen - you join in. Here…." and Deidra grabbed a clean tea towel out of a drawer and threw it at her.

I never saw anyone look more pleased in my life than my aunt did at that moment. Within minutes we were all three chatting away like old friends.

Claire, still worn out by the stress of the past weeks, returned to her room just as soon as she felt it polite to leave. Deidra and family piled up their crockery and disappeared soon after, which left Joe and me chatting beside the fire. I poured us each a glass of Miss Marjorie's best blackberry liqueur, bought at the chapel bring-and-buy. Joe took a sip and choked.

"Should have warned you. The only way the Elliot ladies can get squiffy is by hiding the vodka beneath layers of fruit and sugar. They do a superb apricot too."

He sipped at his drink for a moment staring thoughtfully into the fire.

"Guy wants to come over for a day or two if you don't mind."

"Oh, hell - I don't have another room and I can't ask Deidra to cook more meals! You'll need to stop at the 'Bull'."

"Deidra cooked *that?* Well, waddayaknow," Joe said raising an eyebrow.

"I'm better at digging spuds than mashing them. Why's Guy coming?"

"Mostly because I'm not going back to Bythwaite. You told me to choose. I did. I chose my mother - and by default, you."

I'd assumed his father's remark about Joe's stake in the Bythwaite farm business would pretty much tie him there.

"Of course, that'll cut me out of his Will which is the threat he's holding over me. The reason Guy is coming is because we have a business proposition for you. I'm off to bed now. Sleep well, see you in the morning."

The sun was sinking, throwing a golden halo over the hills. I sat on the front of my battered tractor to watch it. My mood was one of sublime peace. I wouldn't push fate. I'd go to bed.

First thing the following morning I walked my acreage with Dermot and Joe. Most of the conversation was between the two men, but I listened avidly as Dermot discussed fertilizers and crumbled lumps of soil between his fingers knowledgeably.

Joe took over the conversation and discussed the laying in of ash hedging to replace a collapsed wall at the top end of the eight acre field. And so it continued with very little input from me, until we'd walked half a circuit of the entire farm and were more than ready for the spread Deidra had laid out on the kitchen table.

Guy, newly arrived, was drinking from a steaming pint-pot and leafing through a sheaf of papers which he began to fan out on the table.

"Food first," said Joe, sitting down to tea, fresh bread and home-made butter and lemon curd. Deidra would get a proper wage and extra kitchen help, if I could find anyone who'd put up with her.

After we'd eaten our fill, we pushed the pots to one side.

"We've already touched on some of these matters," said my cousin, sorting the papers into order.

"Briefly my idea is this. You have a sizeable arable concern here, and Guy and I have experience in sheep farming, although if we step away from working at Bythwaite and Scarsdale because of Dad, we will have mostly experience to add to the pot - little capital.

"I propose I work with you here. We have discussed the marketing of your produce before. I could help with that - I have the contacts and you're producing quality crops. Selling them shouldn't take too much effort. "

"I could continue to run our tourism business from here…. well not from *here*, obviously," added Guy. "I might eventually have to move elsewhere but Nethershaw could be a step along the way. I could take a small office to work from in the town."

He held up his hand as I began to speak.

"My father is keen I give this a go. He'd like to see me with something of my own. I may have to go back from time to time though to give him a hand if necessary."

"I have some savings," said Joe, "but as most of my capital was reinvested in Bythwaite, it's not nearly enough."

"I could sell some acreage," I offered.

"It might come to that," said Joe, chewing his finger nail. "Let me look around a bit and see if I can come up with an outside investor."

"Might I come with you to Nethershaw tomorrow, Joe?" asked a soft voice from the living room doorway, "Might I come? I won't get in the way, I promise. If I start to be a nuisance, I can always sit in the car and wait."

We all understood what Claire meant.

I was heartbroken for this sweet, kind lady. Her husband had knocked all the stuffing out of her. I supposed there must have been reasons for her circumstances buried somewhere in the past, but as I had no way of knowing what they were, I'd have to try and make the here and now as pleasant as I could for her.

"This afternoon I'd like to get some air if that would be alright. I could go alone if everyone's busy. I know I'm being demanding."

"Would you like to go alone, Claire?"

Her eyes filled with unshed tears.

"No. I... I don't think that would be wise. No perhaps not. I have a book I could read. I could always sit outside."

She looked so disappointed and I could see her thoughts begin to drift away.

"Absolutely you will not! Where would you like to go?"

"To the river, perhaps? It used to be so beautiful. I'd like to see it again."

Joe and I looked at each other over her head. He raised his shoulders. He was as surprised by her statement as I was.

"Do you know the Nethershaw area, Claire?"

"I used to know it well before...." she looked confused and I assumed she had slipped back into her reveries again. Then she seemed to make a supreme effort to rally and said:

"Many years ago when I was young. Many years ago."

She returned to her room before we could question her further.

"No idea," said her son, to my questioning look.

That afternoon, Claire and I strolled down to the river past furrowed fields of greenery. At the end, the path opened directly onto an extensive area of water-washed smooth stones. We took off our shoes, tip-toed across the uneven surface and sat on sheets of flat rock at the water's edge.

Witch Stones

It couldn't have been a more glorious day - hot for early summer. The riverbanks were profuse with king-cups and balsam, and the water dappled with alder. We even saw an iridescent dragon-fly zigzagging its way across a nearby pool.

A kingfisher flashed by, a streak of brilliance against the tumbling water, and unusually for this most reserved of birds, sat on a branch above our heads preening it's gaudy plumage.

It was like bloody Walt Disney. There must be something about this woman which drew all this beauty to her, or perhaps it had always been the same but I hadn't seen it until now. No wonder being incarcerated in that room at Bythwaite had destroyed her spirit.

She twiddled her feet in the water and rested back on out-stretched arms, her face bathed in sunlight. She was quite beautiful and the Grace Kelly look had returned.

"Claire…"

"Hmmm?"

"What happened to keep you in that room at Bythwaite?"

And - in the snap of a finger the mood was gone and she looked frail and distressed again.

"I will tell you one day darling, I promise. But please, not today. Today is too beautiful to spoil with my troubles."

As she slipped back into her private bliss she said:

"I'm not going back to Bythwaite. I'm never going back."

Chapter Twenty-eight

The Mystery of Valerie Mitford-Clarke

The following morning, Joe sat honking his car horn in the yard whilst his mother flapped, trying to juggle her bag, her purse, a set of keys for the house and pull on her cardigan all at the same time.

Honk! Honk! Honk!

She dropped everything on the table, stood at the door and yelled.

"Stop that racket at once, Joseph! I'm being as quick as I can."

Calm collected and in full charge, she slid into the passenger seat beside her son.

Only then did it occur to me she'd come close a time or two but hadn't had a single attack since she'd arrived. I'd even heard her singing to herself that morning in her room.

Without much effort, Guy had found a couple of rooms over one of the shops on Main Street, which once redecorated he thought would do very nicely as an office.

While he and Joe went to discuss the lease with the estate agent, Claire excused herself and wandered off to buy some bits and pieces she'd run short of. It seemed her confidence was returning. She still tired easily, although good food and exercise were clearly having an effect. Our little strolls in the fresh air became longer and longer and Joe relaxed.

I'd told him what she'd said at the river about never going back. I thought Joe was going to cry with relief.

"I'd worried myself sick about her when I made my decision to leave. I was so scared he'd hurt her before we could get away. Can you put up with us for a few months until I can sort out something more permanent? Perhaps she would like to move into Fairview - no, perhaps not," he said, at the expression on my face.

"I saw someone I thought I recognized walking around town," Claire said a day or two later. "At least - obviously I didn't know *him* as such, but he looked just like someone ..... what was the name, now. Scarr? Yes, I'm sure that's right - William Scarr."

"Tony Scarr?" I tried to stop laughing, but in truth the thought of my refined aunt understanding a single word that man uttered was too ridiculous for words.

"It may have been his father or even his grandfather I knew, I suppose. If it was, I couldn't understand a word he said."

I think those weeks were a happy time for us all. Claire unfolded like a flower in the sunny air, Joe relaxed and Guy was excited about setting up his new venture.

My farm was flourishing, thanks to Dermot and his men. Joe had been hiding his light under a bushel when it came to marketing, my customers thought the world of him.

Best of all Uncle Dick stayed at Bythwaite which was a relief for everyone.

But, of course, it was too good to last and it fell apart in the most spectacular way.

My aunt and I had gone to the farmers' market in Nethershaw, and as I was sorting through some tablecloths on one of the stalls, I looked up to see Claire frozen ridged, her eyes wide with shock.

I looked around for the source of her distress, but it was a quiet day and her attention seemed fixed on Valerie Mitford-Clarke who was carrying a laden shopping bag and who was the only other person nearby. I hadn't seen Valerie since the catastrophic day when my testimony had sentenced her husband to prison and I'd made an enemy of her daughter.

Clair dropped to the ground like a stone. I called out to Valerie for help but she'd turned and hurried away in the opposite direction.

Color began to return to my aunt's face and I helped her to her feet.

"Home... take me home," she gasped.

Her stockings torn, and her knee gritty from the fall, she leaned heavily on my arm as I helped her to my car.

Claire had dropped her bag when she'd fallen so I dashed back to pick up her purse, the coins of which had spilled out across the tarmac. A ten-shilling note had lodged beneath her bag and another fluttered off down the road.

I scraped everything together as best I could and returned to the car to find Claire sobbing into her hands.

"Oh, no… no. Not when everything was going so well. Oh no."

"What the hell is going on, Claire?"

"Please, please… just take me back. I never should have come. I never should have left Bythwaite. I shouldn't.. I shouldn't…"

Of course, Joe was in bloody Bradford on a sales trip, and Guy was tarting up his office back in Nethershaw.

Thank God for Deidra and her teapot.

We three sat in my kitchen, two of us distraught, the third looking as if her patience was about to run out.

"What the fuck's going on here? You look like refugees from a gas attack!"

Over the next half hour I had cause to be endlessly grateful for Deidra's acerbic nature.

"What's got your knickers in a twist?" she asked my cultured aunt, ignoring me completely.

"I… I…"

"Spit it out! No-one can help you if you don't."

Robbie picked that exact moment to wander in looking for his mother and exited pronto when she yelled at him to bugger off.

"I can't… I just can't. There are more people involved in this than me and it's all a tissue of lies."

She jumped to her feet and ran for the door, the pair of us hot on her heels. She was getting away so Deidra stuck out her foot and my aunt took her second tumble of the day.

Claire rose slowly to her feet and with dread I saw the familiar glassy gaze had returned to her eyes.

"What's going on NOW!" demanded Deidra.

"My uncle calls it dementia but I think she just panics."

Deirdra drew back her hand and hit Claire across the face hard enough to land her on her back-side again.

"Oh no you don't, you stupid cow. You're not getting out of it that way. They've all been too soft with thee. Tha need a [1]leathering."

As Clair regained her feet, Deidra fetched her a whack to the other cheek. I was utterly amazed to see my aunt's eyes refocus and folding her hand into a fist she hit Deidra in the face. It was her turn to hit the deck.

"That's better," said Deidra, flexing her jaw. "Right. Let's get at that blackberry stuff of Madge Elliot's."

So it was that when Guy reappeared from helping the decorator paint his office, smudged liberally with magnolia paint, he found the three of us launching into the second verse of 'Jerusalem', swinging slopping glasses in unison.

---

[1]*good beating*

Chapter Twenty-nine

An Investment from an Unexpected Source

When I awoke, the dawn sun was just starting to glow through the net curtains. I picked up my pillow which had fallen on the floor, and as I returned it to its proper place, my hand brushed against an envelope.

It was too dark to read and anyway my hangover had given me such a crashing headache I could hardly see, so I dropped whatever it was on the floor and went back to sleep.

I was awoken sometime later by loud voices from Claire's room.

"I'll do what I please. And where did you find this anyway? I knew you'd cause this fuss so I gave it to Meg. You'd no business opening it."

There was a loud masculine sigh of exasperation.

"It was on the floor near her bed. Deidra had come to see her but Meg was still fast asleep. She gave the envelope to me for safe-keeping."

"The money belongs to me, Joseph. Do you understand? I'm your mother and you'll respect my wishes."

My God she sounded determined.

"Right - then we'll get Meg's opinion, she probably knows about it now anyway with all the shouting."

As there was only one other 'she' in the house, that had to be me.

I pulled on my dressing-gown and tip-toed down the landing. Guy was standing with his back against the wall, listening from a safe distance.

"What the hell's going on?" I mouthed.

"Let's find out," said this shy, retiring man overcome with curiosity. He straightened broad shoulders and opened the door. It was there his bravado failed him.

"Good morning to you both," he said inanely. "Anything I can help you with?"

Joe gave the letter to him and turned away to the window, one hand in his pocket the other raking through his hair.

I looked round Guy's arm and nearly choked. He held a banker's draft for fifty thousand pounds made out to Joseph Graham and signed by Claire Armstrong Graham.

"Fifty fucking thousand!" I exclaimed, gobsmacked.

"It's too much, Mother," said Joe still staring out of the window.

"Good God, Claire - have you lost your mind? Why would you give Joe fifty thousand? I wouldn't give him fifty!" I said aghast.

The mood lightened, as they all began to laugh at me.

"I'm giving him nothing," said Claire. "It's a business transaction. I want to be a shareholder in Ghyll Howe."

"Now I understand why your son looks so bewildered - you could buy the whole bloody farm for fifty thousand."

"I don't want to buy the farm. I want to put you on a firm business footing. I'm not going back to Bythwaite. This is what I want," she finished firmly.

It was Guy who first recognized the implications of added investment to finance our new business venture, but he was wary.

"Are you certain about this Mrs. Graham? Your husband will try to stop you any way he can."

"I'd like to see him try. The money is mine, inherited directly from my grandfather. Under the terms of his Will, I am his sole legatee. There's considerably more than fifty-thousand so I won't suffer, even if you make a complete mess of it, which I'm positive you won't."

Joe sat on the bed and took Claire's hand.

"Does Dad know about all this?" he asked earnestly.

"He doesn't know about grandfather's estate - I told him nothing. It's none of his business."

She smiled maliciously.

"Now if you don't mind, I'm tired and don't want to talk about this anymore. Tomorrow… we'll discuss it more tomorrow before we call the lawyers in."

Guy stood on the landing still holding the draft in his hand and examined it carefully.

"I don't suppose Claire would give us a forgery," I said.

Joe, whose thoughts had taken quite a different direction, pondered:

"This means between us we could own a sizeable chunk of Westmoreland."

This was just ridiculous. Ten years ago I was a 'scrow' from Fairview, the butt of children's jokes. Since, I had dragged myself, through God's good grace and damned hard work, to a position of some consequence in the local farming community.

I'd become acquainted with family I'd known of vaguely - some for better and some for worse - and I'd become friends with the Greenwoods.

Now my aunt had made me a gift of one-third of fifty thousand pounds. The heavens surely were smiling down on Margaret Graham, and as if to confirm my fortune, a beautiful red butterfly fluttered through the open window and settled on my shoulder. I moved my hand to put it outside again, but it flew to my finger where it sat for a moment opening and closing its lovely wings before floating back outside.

'Got ter specerlate t' acoomerlate' as Dermot very rightly observed. Well - we were about to 'accomerlate' and the bloody 'specerlating' was scaring the shit out of me. It didn't exactly fill me with confidence that my two business partners looked even more thunderstruck than I.

"Well - what do we do now?" I asked, my elation disappearing out of the window with the butterfly.

"I don't know about you," said Joe repeating his mantra, "but I'm going for a pint.

Chapter Thirty

The Ups, Downs and Shocks of Richard Graham

Claire and I had become used to our strolls and on sunny days, we would wander along the river bank or climb the sweeping slopes of a lonely hillside. Sometimes I would pack up a picnic and at others we would drop into a local inn.

But things had changed since she made her generous investment and, instead of my friend, I began to think of her as more of a business partner. I didn't want that - it put a barrier between us. She felt it too.

"I'd thought to make things easier for you but it seems I've just made you uncomfortable," Claire worried, "I'm sorry but even if I could, I'm not sure I would want to take the money back. It's a tool, a means to an end. We have to make it work for us. We might fall flat on our faces - we may become millionaires, who knows? In the meantime we'll have to find a way to be comfortable with it."

We were sharing confidences again but on another level. That we were niece and aunt had taken second place to teacher and acolyte - and friend once more.

Eventually, Uncle Dick did get wind of happenings at Ghyll Howe, and late one afternoon as Claire, Guy, Joe and I were taking our break sitting on the yard fence, his Land Rover swerved to a halt in front of us.

"Get in this damn car, Claire. NOW."

He'd clearly expected her to beg his forgiveness and go back to Bythwaite, but instead Claire, looking like a very determined apparition, said:

"I will do no such thing, Richard."

He pulled Claire from the fence by the arm and began dragging her towards the car.

"Not one penny of my money'll be used on this pile of shit."

His disdainful gaze encompassed my whole property.

There were bright red fingermarks where he'd gripped Claire's arm and I ran to support her as her knees buckled.

"Get back in that vehicle and off my land, Uncle Dick. You're not welcome here - you will NEVER be welcome here again."

"Get in the car Claire - we're going home," he threatened.

Dick grabbed her arm again, and landed on his backside on one of my chickens which took off behind the barn in high dudgeon. For a split second I was too distracted by the clamor to notice what'd happened.

My lovely cousin Joe, usually the essence of kindness and consideration had fetched his father a left to the jaw which had knocked him for six. There lay Uncle Dick, hair coated in chicken shit, out for the count with a trickle of blood running from the corner of his mouth.

"Get her to her room Meg, before he comes round," said Joe. "Think you can manage the stairs?"

"I'll help," offered Guy who had to that moment been try-ing to keep out of the way, assuming it was a family ar-gument which of course it had been.

I was at once shocked, amazed and truth to tell, a bit scared. I hadn't thought Joe capable of losing control. I'd been so furious with him when he hadn't defended his mother's wish to stay with me.

"Be careful, Joe - he might not be in the best of moods when he comes round," I grinned.

Once I'd got Claire to her bed, pulled up the coverlet and Guy and I had returned to the yard, Joe had dragged his dad into the driver's seat of his Land Rover and shoved the keys into his limp hand.

Dick was just beginning to stir as we slammed shut the kitchen door and flopping back against it laughed with re-lief listening to my uncle's fruitless yells from outside.

"You fool Joseph. You've given away your birthright to a woman who only owns the clothes she stands up in - and I bought her those. Ask the whore why she's been confined to that room for so many years. You just ask her!"

There was the sound of an engine revving and my uncle left. I just hoped there wouldn't be Barber-sized pancakes decorating the dirt on the lane.

"I'd like to see your mother alone first Joe if that'll be okay. I know you must be worried sick. I won't be long, I promise."

He had spent his entire life in terror of Richard Graham's temper, and now he'd made a firm decision, things looked about to change. It must have been bewildering.

I'd expected to find Claire in bed sleeping off her distress, but she'd washed and changed. She'd dragged a small armchair to the window and was gazing out at hills adrift with scudding shadows.

She didn't turn as I entered so I began to think there was substance to my fear that the confrontation with Dick had undone all the good work of the past weeks.

She'd had no recurrence of her anguish since we'd seen Valerie Mitford-Clarke in Nethershaw, and even then she'd pulled herself together pretty quickly.

I should have had more faith in the healing air of Ghyll Howe perhaps.

Claire turned to me slowly, her eyes brimming with tears and her face ashen.

"You have been so good to me and I've been the cause of such misery. The connection between the Graham brothers and the Armstrong sisters is a complicated one."

Suddenly her voice and manner changed.

"Shall we be seeing Mrs. Elsom, Mama? You did promise.... You did, Mama," she wheedled.

I was so startled I took several steps towards the door, but then adopting a confidence I didn't feel, replied:

130

"Of course, my dear. Come now - time to sleep. We'll discuss it some more in the morning," and I ushered her to her bed to rest.

When Joe looked in on her later, she'd crept under the eider-down and was fast asleep.

Bright and early the following morning Claire was arranging blooms in an earthenware jug and beaming happily at me. She remembered not one thing about her absence of the previous day. I didn't tell Joe for fear of upsetting him - after all it was such a rare slip.

I don't know if what happened next was as a result of Richard Graham's fury, Claire's act of independence which I'd been responsible for, or just Dick's sheer bloody-mindedness at being thwarted.

Guy had returned to his office and Joe had gone to Coniston straight after breakfast to finish tying things up prior to their first booking.

Claire, Deidra and I were looking over some lettuce Dermot's wife had planted the week before:

"Bastard slugs - I've used near half a box of salt and the damn things are still chomping away. Lettuces have more holes in them than Ma Wilson's macramé," she scowled.

Uncle Dick's Land Rover swerved so hard into the yard and pulled up so sharply it skidded, hit a concrete wall at the side of the [1]midden and rolled over, flinging my uncle's jacket, assorted boxes and a pair of muddy wellies

[1]*manure heap*

violently about the cab.

Claire ran to help out of instinct but I held her back, mindful of our last

encounter with Uncle Dick. There was no holding Deidra though.

With some difficulty she wrenched open the damaged driver's side door and began dragging Dick out of the car.

He leapt to his feet, beet-red, and began pummeling her about the head with his fists until she fell, blooded and beaten and for once speechless on the concrete of the yard.

I looked from face to face in disbelief.

Uncle was hefting himself to his feet, swearing like a trooper and dusting detritus from his clothes. He made straight for me, arms akimbo, face contorted with hate.

BANG!

Deidra and I jumped round to see Clair, the weight of a smoking shotgun supported on the top rail of the fence, standing shaken but resolute, staring at her husband. Or perhaps it might have been more accurate to say her ex-husband since Richard Graham was laid spread-eagled on the ground with a neat black hole between his eyes. He looked calmer than I'd ever seen him.

"Damn!" said Deidra. "Great shot!"

Chapter Thirty-one

Dastardly Dick and the Day in Court

When Joe arrived in the yard just as the gun went off, he was confronted by a frozen montage of figures. Typically only Deidra was moving. She'd heaved herself to her feet and was in the process of prizing Claire's fingers gently away from the trigger of my Ejector shotgun,

Dick Graham, quiet and non-threatening probably for the first time ever, had a pool of black blood spreading from the back of his head and soaking into the sawdust of the farmyard.

Looking back, it was perhaps surprising that no-one made a move to check him over but left him seeping, while we rushed to Claire.

Far from being the wilting violet everyone took her for, she was standing four-square looking down at her husband of thirty years with a smile of grim satisfaction on her face.

She turned to me and said:

"Will you need help?" I shook my head, speechless.

"Then let's go back to Beckton Joe. As the new owner of Bythwaite you need to get things into your own hands. We'll be back next week Meg. We've a business transaction to complete."

I'd never seen this side of Claire before. The crime she'd committed didn't seem to have permeated her consciousness at all. She was totally in control and seemed to have added ten years to her life. When I finally found my voice again I said:

"I've already been witness to one murder in Nethershaw. They have me cast as an accessory as it is. Go home."

"Aye," said Deidra, considering her own future, "This'll knock macramé into a cocked hat at the WI."

"We can't just leave and let Meg face the police alone," said Joe appalled.

"I've just to report it," I said. "They've got the body and no doubt someone'll be across to pick Claire up sooner or later.

"I'll explain the situation to Bob Ryder. He'll have to get on to his HQ at Penrith - I just hope they don't send that twit Fernside. We don't need him doing his 'Dragnet' impression round Nethershaw again."

Still no-one had taken notice of Uncle Dick.

Joe hadn't even looked at his dad and I saw him nudge his mother away before she gave him a hefty kick on her way past. The pain she'd borne all those years was being released in a rush of anger she was finding hard to control.

When she got to Joe's car and was about to open the door, Claire turned to me and said:

"I couldn't let him harm you, Meg dear. It was you or him. He had to go."

She got in the car and she and her son disappeared down the track to the road.

Dermot flung a spud sack over the body before the other laborers saw him. Then he sent them all home.

"Deidra, take Miss Graham inside. To hell with the tea - get her a stiff drink," he ordered.

I got a 'stiff tea'.

It was Dermot who rang Bob Ryder and told him to come on his own and without anyone knowing.

He turned up in his battered Hillman with its defunct blue light.

"What's all this then?" he said. "Why the secrecy?"

Dermot moved the corner of the sack away with the toe of his boot.

"Who's this?" said Bob, squatting down and taking a good professional look.

"It's my uncle," I explained, "Dick… Richard Graham. He owns - owned - Bythwaite Farm at Beckton."

Still no-one had shown the least interest in his demise.

"Oh," said Bob scratching his head, "What's he doing here then?"

"His wife shot him. She was staying with me, but she's gone home."

"Oh," said Bob again. "You realize I'm going to have to call this in, don't you Miss Graham?"

It seems they specialized in clueless coppers at Penrith nick. The one they sent arrested me and Dermot and did his best with Deidra but that was always going to be a losing battle.

And so it came about I found myself in the dock of another court, facing the same judge as the first time round.

I'd no idea why he remembered me but remember me he did. He leaned over his desk and fixed me with a beady eye:

"What? You again? You're getting to be a regular fixture in my court. What do you want this time. Not another murder I take it."

This was stretching it a bit. I'd only been once before and that was ages ago.

"As a matter of fact, it is, Your Honor," I said politely.

"Regular little Lizzie Borden, aren't you."

The trial continued over a couple of weeks. It dragged on then finished abruptly when they couldn't find a character witness for Uncle Dick and the majority of those called seemed to think his death not a bad idea.

His Lordship had been pretty miffed with Claire at the beginning. He'd had to send Bob Ryder to pick her up from Beckton, but once he'd met her he was inclined to be magnanimous. She was, after all, a lady through and through - even though she spoke with a Lancashire accent.

I have no doubt at all she beguiled the judge with the innocent charm of a Grace Kelly, even if she'd blasted a hole through the head of her spouse.

In the end she was found guilty of manslaughter by reason of provocation, and the judge bound her over to keep the peace for five years in the full knowledge she'd only shot the one husband and he, by all accounts, deserved every-thing he got.

Chapter Thirty-two

Burial and Bonfire at Beckton

So that was that. A generation of the Grahams of Bythwaite Farm was now gone. One under a sheep on the fells above Fairview and the other in a welter of blood in a farmyard near Nethershaw.

Uncle Dick was buried in the yard of a church he'd never darkened the door of except for 'hatch, match and dispatch'. It was a brief ceremony, poorly attended. Josh Greenwood came over from Scarsdale which I thought was good of him. Guy, of course, was there for Joe.

As the sods sounded against the wood of the coffin, the faces of Joe and his mother revealed nothing of their thoughts. The gravestone read:

Richard Graham 1908 - 1959
Son of Mary Carrick Graham and Joseph Graham
Died as the result of an accident.

No word of love or even affection, a life wasted on bile and spite.

Meanwhile in the Nethershaw pubs my laborers who hadn't seen a thing, had become celebrities giving contradictory stories about happenings at Ghyll Howe. I sometimes stood in the shadows, glass in hand and chuckled as a simple shooting in a farmyard turned into the 'Gunfight at the OK Corral' with Dermot as Wyatt Earp.

Witch Stones

Claire stopped being Grace Kelly and turned into Boudicca overnight.

On my next visit to Bythwaite, it was to find a heap of furniture at one side of the yard, piled up for burning. There were a couple of elderly chairs, a mattress and an ugly nineteen-twenties coffee table amongst various smaller items. They were pretty much beaten up and stuck into the ground next to them was an axe, its handle worn smooth from many years use.

Claire was sitting in Uncle Dick's office systematically emptying all the folders from his filing cabinets and re-sorting them, occasionally flinging a discarded sheet into a waste paper basket.

"Hello Margaret, dear," she smiled. "Joe's over at Scarsdale. He'll be back this evening with Guy. They've to go over…. something or other."

She distractedly scanned a particular paper, then screwed it up and threw it away.

"Margaret? Why Margaret? I've been Meg since I was seventeen."

"If you're to be a serious business woman, it's important you have a serious name. You'll need to practice a signature as well - for cheques, contracts and the like. What do you think of a middle initial? Margaret W Graham sound so much grander, don't you think?"

A thought occurred to her and she backtracked.

"What were you before and why did you become Meg?"

Witch Stones

"I was always Maggie growing up, but when I went to work for Mrs. Mitford-Clarke she said it sounded like a sheepdog and christened me Meg after the girl in 'Little Women'"

"You worked for that woman?"

"Why? What's wrong with her?"

"You do know her maiden name, don't you?"

"No - why should I? She's always been Valerie Mitford-Clarke to me. I'd never thought of her as anything else."

She considered me for a moment through delicate gold rimmed glasses then returned to her task.

"Is that it? What's wrong with her and what's her maiden name? And how do you know what it is, in any case?"

She broke off the conversation and called out:

"Sarah…. bring us some tea - and some of your mum's scones. They're in a tin in the pantry - second shelf, left."

"Right you are, Mrs. Claire. Back in a mo."

As we settled down to scones and tea, I asked:

"Well, are you going to tell me or not?"

"I think 'not' has to be the answer - just at the moment."

When first we'd met, I'd been introduced to a quaint timid lady on the verge of a nervous breakdown. Now she was an organized business woman with a confident manner.

We finished our snack, Claire stacked the remaining papers onto the desk and we left the awful dusty office.

"Come on. You can help me turn out my room. Not one stick of furniture will remain. The lot goes on the bonfire."

Before we removed the furniture, she went through the drawers, removing clothing, photographs, bottles of medication and perfume and other paraphernalia clearly collected over many years.

In the top drawer of her sideboard from where she'd removed the photograph of herself with my mother and their brother on our first meeting, she withdrew a worn shoe-box of assorted pictures. Tucked away at the very back of the drawer was a silver repoussé frame holding the picture of a young man.

She polished it lovingly with the sleeve of her cardigan then abruptly returned to the sitting-room where she carefully put it in place of honor on the mantlepiece.

"Handsome, don't you think?" she said, head on one side.

Indeed he was; tall and straight, with eyes that looked from the picture into those of the viewer. He'd the appearance of a Keats or Wordsworth - noble and romantic; a face to fall in love with.

"He looks vaguely familiar," I said pensively. "He has a look of Joe about him, I suppose. Uncle Dick too."

She laughed and walked round the room collecting all the pictures of Uncle Dick and throwing them into a waste bin - even the ones taken on their wedding day. All memory of Richard Graham was being systematically expunged.

"Here, Sarah," she said loudly. "Put these on the bonfire."

"Righty-ho."

The larger pictures from the box she laid out neatly on the coffee table.

"I must buy some more frames - then I can hang these."

I noticed that several of the likenesses were less formal shots of the same young man from the ornate frame.

"Who *is* that Claire?" I said pointing at an apparent holiday snap of the man laughing and with his trousers rolled up to the knees. On a shop behind was a barely discernable sign 'Boulanger et Pâtissier'.

"I'm surprised you don't recognize him, Margaret. Have a guess. He does have a look of Joe, doesn't he?"

I took one of the pictures and sat in a chair to consider it. He was so familiar - like the image of an uncle or grandfather from long ago in my childhood.

"I'll leave you to it. Now I've sorted it out, I'd better make a start on cleaning that filthy office."

I picked up the rest of the pictures and took them over to the window to view them in a better light.

There was another image of the same young man in World War Two uniform. He was sitting in a canvas folding chair and grinning straight at the camera.

"Oh shit!" I yelled. "It's Dad!"

"Took you long enough," came a voice from the hall.

I hadn't recognized him mostly because I remembered him with a permanently worried frown, thin and drawn.

That this handsome man with the carefree smile could be my father was almost beyond belief. This was a Robert Graham I'd never dreamed existed.

"Can I look at the rest?"

"Help yourself."

Some of the pictures looked to have been taken with a Box Brownie so were too tiny to make out. The bigger ones had names and places written on the back - some also had dates.

Joe and Guy chose that moment to come bowling in, laughing and joking.

"The Grahams aren't from these parts," said Joe, looking over my shoulder at the photograph of my dad. "They were reivers in the days of Good Queen Bess."

Chapter Thirty-three

Claire, the Seven Sisters and a White-out

I knew reivers were the equivalent of the mafia, running protection rackets by terror in the Scottish border areas of long ago, but nothing else. Joe laughed at the expression on my face.

"Can't you picture me racing across the Cumbrian mountains on my charger, bloody sword aloft?"

He struck a pose to that effect and I burst out laughing.

"Our grandmother was a Carrick - they were aristocrats of sorts. A Lord Carrick generations back was tasked with keeping peace on the March, which was the western end of the border."

Joe picked up one of the professionally posed shots.

"Here she is. Mary Carrick Graham - Molly. I never knew her, of course. She died years before I was born, but Mum knew her well - they were great friends."

Written on the back in script was

Molly Carrick and Joseph Graham
on the occasion of their engagement.
April 23rd 1906

And stamped on the front in gold letters:

J.J. Laidlaw, King Street, Carlisle.

The diamond on Mary's finger was held at an angle the better to catch the light. She looked like the cat that got the cream. Joseph Graham must have been quite a catch, although I have to say he didn't look a barrel of laughs to me.

"Ah, I see you've found Molly and Joseph," said Claire. "They got married in Carlisle and came down here straight after and bought Bythwaite. They're both buried in the churchyard.

"Your father was always Molly's favorite. Handsome and debonair, kind and gentle. Richard was so jealous of him. He took after his dad. No humor."

She smiled a little secret smile, glanced up at the picture on the mantle, then shook a grubby yellow duster out of a nearby window and clapped her hands free of dust. A look of distaste crossed her face:

"That office hasn't been cleaned in thirty years."

Her dumping of her husband, then putting him on his back with a bullet through his brow, certainly should have been stressful, but she'd turned her attention to Guy and was chatting away. She seemed as far from one of her attacks as I'd ever seen her.

Later that afternoon, thinking a little alone time might do me good, I took a hike in the fresh air up to the Sisters. A bracing wind bent the reeds horizontal in a nearby marshy field and a curlew cried eerily from a distant moor.

I wasn't expecting company but found Claire sitting with her back against the largest stone, gazing unseeingly across the valley, deep in thought. Her expression was hard to gauge. There was nothing of joy in it, nor even of sorrow, just a terrible longing and hopelessness which disappeared in a flash as she caught sight of me.

"Hello dear. I wasn't expecting company but it's lovely to see you. Here, come and sit down. I was just thinking what a strange place this is. The Stones do sing after a fashion, don't they?"

I was struck by the same feeling of unease, of buzzing, I'd experienced on my visit with Guy. We sat in silence for a few moments before she kissed my cheek and said:

"Come on, dear. It's freezing cold and you've only a cardigan on. Let's go home.

It had indeed been cold and from that point on the weather worsened and became more wintery by the day.

Stinging hail had given way to large flakes of snow with rapidly increasing drifts on the higher ridges.

Joe paid a quick visit to Fairview and Coniston to batten down the hatches of his properties.

Bythwaite was a large farm, well adapted for any demands of weather, but Scarsdale was another matter and I hadn't forgotten the tale of Guy's appendicitis.

When he hadn't heard from his friend for a while, Joe asked around and was told the telephone lines were down and we'd hear no more until they could be fixed when the weather improved.

I went home while I could. Dermot wouldn't need me - the severity of the weather would mean he'd be working

146

on maintenance and repairs for a while, but some of my smaller customers might be suffering, so I'd have to load up whatever was left in storage and do my best to get it out to them.

Guy's office in Nethershaw was locked but hadn't been packed away so I went and did that first, warmed myself before the roaring fire in the Lion and went home feeling depressed.

My cousin and aunt were lost to me for the foreseeable future and my good friend was out of the picture. The best I could hope for were tales of derring-do in the pub, about stalwart farmers digging prize ewes out of drifts, and how they'd survived disaster by cuddling up for warmth.

Being a sheep farmer's daughter, the derring-do passed me by completely and I was left wondering what live-stock from the sheep they'd be digging out of their hair for the next few weeks.

Chapter Thirty-four

Christmas and Devastation for Guy

It being the Festive Season, Deidra had pulled out all the stops. That woman was a saint, if a tainted one.

When I got back from Nethershaw, she'd had a seven foot Christmas tree erected in my parlor and her kids, laughing and joking, were hanging not only the usual baubles, but paper-chains and decorations they'd made with their mother.

Along the mantle-shelf and door jambes were long strands of variegated ivy, its white edges painted with glue and dipped in silver glitter. Brightly colored paper Chinese lanterns were hanging from the rafters and there was a large bowl of chestnuts, cut and ready for roasting on the hearth.

In all my life I'd never seen a Christmas like it. But there was more.... on the table steamed a dressed goose, skin crisp, moist gravy oozing from beneath. Roast potatoes, parsnips and carrots and all the fare of a splendid dinner.

"And you needn't think that's all for you," Deidra said. "Pull her a chair up Sean. Dermot, slice the goose. Paul get Miss Graham some taties, here's a spoon."

Dermot had a look of Bob Cratchet about him and I wondered if there was a 'pudding in the copper' and Martha was about to pop out of the woodwork.

Martha didn't... but the Barber brats did. They turned up in a snow-storm singing the first verses of all the carols they knew, which amounted to 'The First Noel', 'Twinkle, Twinkle Little Star' - not a carol but well intentioned said Deidra - and 'Silent Night', which had become anything but, since Angelique Barber had good lungs. Once they'd finished they started from the beginning again because we'd yet to open the door. When we finally did, hands were firmly stuck out palms up, and a rapid chorus of [1]'We wis' yer an 'appy Crismus' was galloped through.

Thinking it money well spent, I gave them each a shilling, which was greeted with:

"Cor blimey - if I'd knowd it were that easy I'd a' gone every Sund'y," said John-Claude.

"You can't do that, [2]yer berk. It's only Crismus then you've to wait 'nother year."

[3]"Poor show fer a twelve-month then," he whittled as they crunched off through the snow.

Of course, the Christmas the O'Connor family had blessed me with had come as a complete surprise, so I was very embarrassed to have nothing to give them in return.

"You don't give God's good grace at Christmas with hope of return. What good'd that do?" said Dermot when I apologized, and his wife nodded.

But I couldn't let it go. What didn't they have? They needed very little - they'd a home, Dermot had a good job getting better by the year, and they had each other. They were the kind of people who needed little else. There was nothing I could do now but I'd think on it long and hard. It wasn't entirely philanthropic - it would give me such

[1]*We wish you a Happy Christmas*
[2]*you idiot*
[3]*Not much good for a year then*

pleasure to return the favor.

The solution came on a New Years Eve, quiet and festive-free. I was dozing before a dying fire when I jumped to my feet. What didn't they have? Yes! Free time together. I'd give Dermot time off and send the whole family to Morecambe for a week in the summer. They hadn't had a holiday since they'd been with me.

When I mentioned this to Deidra she was offended.

"I didn't stand there cooking you're fuckin' dinner with a view to recompense - cheeky mare!"

"For once in your life [1]put a sock in it Deidra! Tell the kids it's a birthday present."

"Tough job there since the twins were born in February and Robbie in April. Don't be so daft."

"Deidra - you will go to the seaside!" *Cinderella you will go to the ball?* "Just bear in mind for once in your life who pays whose wages round here. You're bloody-well going!"

She burst into tears. It was disconcerting.

I'd tried to ring Claire and Joe over Christmas, but the telephone lines must have been out of action to Bythwaite as well. It was early February before I spoke to them, and that was only because there had been a temporary break in the bad weather, and the telephone lineman from Kendal had managed to get through with help from one of the local farmers.

[1]*shut your mouth*

Everyone at Bythwaite was fine and I understood they'd been treated to 'Rockin' Around the Christmas Tree' for three solid weeks. Sarah had decided Connie was a bit downbeat for Christmas and adopted Brenda Lee instead.

Joe still hadn't heard from Guy but accepted it was early days. Although the Bythwaite phone was in working order, it was unlikely the one at Scarsdale had been fixed yet.

When he still hadn't heard from Guy by the middle of February, Joe decided to take one of the tractors and see if he could get through himself. It appeared to me that had that been possible, Guy would already have made contact.

Claire was frantic for Joe's safety. She used every argument she could to dissuade him from going. She even resorted to the 'you will leave your poor old mother all alone' moan which, obviously Joe ignored. She'd already proved she could run a farm and control Brenda Lee.

But finally Joe did get through, taking the lineman on the back of his tractor.

Hours of careful driving later, he'd pulled into the yard at Scarsdale, with the cleats in the tractor's wheels crammed with compacted snow. All looked as neat and pristine as a Victorian Christmas card. The sheep down from the fells had begun digging through the snow to the grass beneath, and the racks had been stocked with hay.

What Joe discovered inside came as a shattering shock. Out of Guy's hearing he recounted the following tale to his mother and me.

Josh had sent the servants and farmworkers home when the weather began to worsen, which was standard practice. There had just been himself, Guy and Mrs. Beattie, the housekeeper who knew no other home, when the worst winter in living memory broke.

Joe banged the snow from his boots and crossed the threshold of the farmhouse, shouting his friend's name.

He found Guy warming his hands before a meagre kitchen fire, unshaven, unwashed and unshorn, eyes dull and uncomprehending.

It had always been a cold house anyway, with its slate floors and thick stone walls, but it had become freezing, its small windows encrusted with ice on the inside. The only warm place was the square footage where Guy huddled.

At first his friend appeared dazed from the cold, so Joe lifted him by the shoulders and shook him. Eventually his swollen eyes focused then filled with tears. His head drooped and he sobbed, only standing because Joe was holding him upright.

"What the hell's happened Guy?" said Joe giving him another shake.

Guy stood unsteadily and wove his way between the furniture to the dark hall. At the end was a wide carpeted stairway which split after a dozen steps and led left and right to the two wings of the house. On the little landing between, laying with her head tipped back over the first downward stair, lay the twisted body of the Greenwood family housekeeper Doris Beattie, with a bloody cut to her brow. There was no disguising she was dead, nor that she had been for some considerable time. That her remains were in such good condition was owing to the cold. She was frozen stiff, her lashes and hair rimed with ice.

Joe ushered Guy back into the kitchen and stoked the fire high with the remaining logs on the hearth. He took off his coat and wrapped it round his friend's shoulders. Only then did he realize he'd forgotten to ask after Josh.

"Where's your Dad?"

Guy, who still hadn't spoken, drew Joe's coat around his shoulders, and heading outside crunched off across the snow towards the ruins of the old manor, with its corner of corrugated iron roof.

Inside, Guy shifted some of the feed with his foot to reveal a door in the floor and motioned for Joe to open it.

The door hid a large brick-lined drop to what presumably was a cellar belonging to the old manor. It was too dark to see inside.

Joe slammed the door shut. If Josh was down there, he was beyond help.

"We have to get you back to Bythwaite, Guy. You need warming up, then you can start at the beginning and tell me what's happened."

Chapter Thirty-five

Bythwaite Regained: Guy Turns to Me for Help

Back at Bythwaite, Claire was like a cat on hot bricks.

I sat her down with drinks ranging from tea to brandy until late afternoon when the phone rang.

She leapt from her chair and snatched up the receiver in the hall before the caller could ring off.

"Yes? Yes! Oh, thank God Joe! Are you alright?"

I couldn't hear Joe's reply of course, only a murmur.

"Yes… yes. I'll get right on it. But what's happened? Do I need to make up a room for Josh as well? Is it so bad up there?"

But Joe had already gone.

Claire and I opened up one of the guest-rooms, put fresh linen on the bed and lit a fire in the grate. She pulled shut the heavy velvet curtains to keep the warmth in the room, cold from standing empty.

"Sarah - tell your mother to put some soup on. Mr. Joseph is on his way back with Mr. Greenwood. They'll need something hot."

I also banked up the sitting-room fire until the room glowed with its warmth. Still it was a good two hours before we saw the lights of the tractor turn into the yard, by which time it was dark.

There was a fine snow falling, whipped up by a blustery wind when I reached the tractor.

"Get inside, Meg and turn back the bed - I need to get him straight upstairs. There're a couple of old stone hot water bottles in the broom-cupboard I think. Get Sarah to fill them and wrap them in towels."

With some difficulty - Guy was a large man and a heavy load even for Joe - he was placed in the warm soft bed, the blankets pulled up to his chin. I took the bottles from Sarah and slipped them into the foot-end of the bed. The sudden warmth caused Guy to stiffen with pain.

"He'll be alright now. We'll leave him alone for a while to come to," said Joe.

Later Claire, Joe and I sat round the fire in the sitting room, while Sarah brought us hot chocolate and a plate of [1]mock crab sandwiches.

"Put your coat on Sarah and fetch some eggs from the run. Your mother'll need some for baking," said Joe in an instantly foiled attempt to remove Sarah.

"Lost yer wits, Joe?" said his servant with derision. "'ens don't lay eggs int' snow."

"Mr. Joseph," said Claire, absently, swilling the last of her chocolate round in her cup and waving her away. Sarah tutted and left.

"I warn you now what I'm about to say will shock you. I'm sorry about that but it's best to get it over with while Guy's not here."

We were really not prepared for the tragedy which unf-

[1]*A spread composed of cheese, tomatoes and breadcrumbs invented during the food shortages of WW2*

olded; how Joe had found his friend half-dead from cold, their housekeeper frozen on the stairs with a broken neck, and his father's dead body thrown into what appeared to be an old ice house.

"What do we do for him? It'll scar him for life. How long has he been living there with two corpses?" I asked.

"No idea," said Joe, warming his posterior against the fire. "He wasn't exactly in a state for explanations."

"Move Joe," said his mother. "You're blocking the heat."

I crept upstairs periodically to bank up the fire and tuck the blankets round Guy's body. As he warmed up, he slowly began to come round and started to shiver. This time I doubted it had much to do with the

cold.

After that, we took it in turns sitting with him. He wasn't left alone for a moment. None of us wanted him to awaken to a strange room.

For my part, I rubbed his hand between mine and sang a chorus of 'Que Sera Sera' to raise my spirits if no-one else's.

Sarah had brought me a cup of tea.

[1]"Here y'are Meg. Cuppa char. Shall I fetch one for Guy as well or in't 'e up to it yet?" and at my look of disbelief, [2]"Righty-oh, I'll be off then."

[1]*Here you are, Meg. A cup of tea. Shall I fetch one for Guy too or isn't he up to it yet?*
[2]*Okay, I'll go then.*

Witch Stones

She slammed the door behind her which woke Guy up.

He was still in the same state he'd been in when Joe'd found him. His clothes, skin and hair were filthy, his beard over-grown. He clung to my hand like a drowning man and I kissed his forehead.

"Can I get you anything?" I whispered.

He pulled my head down and kissed me gently on the lips.

"Just be here for a little while," he rasped.

It was nearly midnight when I returned to the sitting-room. Claire and Joe sat one either side of the fireplace, and looked up expectantly as I entered the room.

"He came round briefly," I told Claire, "then fell back asleep again. He asked me not to leave so I'd better go back, but I wanted to tell you both to go to bed. There's no point in waiting up. I'll call you if there's any significant change."

"Will you be alright dear?" asked Claire, concerned. "You've already been up there for two hours."

"Go, you too Joe. Good night."

Chapter Thirty-six

The Tragedy of Scarsdale Manor Farm

When I returned to Guy's room, he was awake and gazing into the embers of the fire. I sat down on the bed.

"Are you feeling better?"

"Come here," he whispered and snuggled down with me in his arms. He rested his cheek against my hair and sighed.

I stood it for as long as I could, but then recoiled at his body odor.

"Can I get you a bowl of water so you can wash?"

"That bad?" he replied and his tone was bitter.

"You have no idea! I'll fetch Joe."

It was two in the morning, but Joe helped Guy bathe then shaved him. I cut his hair after a fashion. I was put in mind of Miss Dent lopping my long hair to get rid of the nits when I first ventured down from the fells.

Wrapped in one of Joe's warm robes Guy sat pensive before the bedroom fire.

"Okay! Spit it out," said Joe with the lack of tact born of life-long friendship. "I'll go and dig Mother out of bed so you don't have to go through it twice."

As I was just about to open my mouth, Joe frowned at me and said:

"Don't you think, now the phones are working, you ought to contact Dermot about the farm. You might be ruined and my mother would have nothing to invest in."

In other words - *push off.*

"If you think I'm ringing Dermot at four in the morning you're off your trolley. It'll be tomorrow."

I'm staying.

But I did give them a little space by going to wake Claire. She'd been listening to our voices for some time, although she couldn't hear what we were saying.

"Is Guy alright?" she asked, rolling her hair round her fingers and fixing it atop her head with hairgrips from her nightstand.

"He's a lot better - Joe helped him wash and shave and I butchered his hair. He's not exactly Hollywood but he looks infinitely better than he did. No. It's a look in his eyes I've never seen before. He looks almost….."

I searched for a word I couldn't find and ended up with 'feral'. That wasn't it but it was along those lines.

"Has he eaten?" asked Claire and when I shrugged she clicked her tongue at me impatiently as she cinched the belt of her robe.

Claire led Guy to the chintz chair by the sitting room fire and brought a crocheted blanket to wrap over his knees. He was beginning to look a bit red in the face, and I wondered if the human body was designed to take such extremes of temperature in such a short time.

I whipped the blanket away and Guy looked at me with gratitude.

The point in time had come when he was no longer able to avoid the inevitable.

"Dad slipped on the ice on the front steps and broke his arm. Mrs. Beattie and I managed to get him into bed."

Guy began to shiver violently despite the stifling room but pushed me away when I laid a comforting hand on his arm. I saw him steel himself to continue.

"His arm was shattered rather than broken, and despite Mrs. Beattie's constant care, Dad developed blood poisoning and the wound turned septic. Penicillin would have fixed it easily but we were snowed in, so had only Mrs. Beattie's home remedies to rely on."

He turned to me, took my hand and said earnestly:

"Why did I recover Meg, and Dad didn't? Why?"

"How did she fix your appendicitis? Did she do anything out of the ordinary?"

"I don't remember much - I was only ten. I do remember Mrs. Beattie wiping my stomach with orange paste and Dad clamping my head under his arm while he poured whisky down my throat, and the agony of it all, but the rest is a blur."

"Turmeric," said Claire knowledgeably. "Best natural antiseptic known to man. And whisky does a pretty good job as anesthetic."

"That you survived at all is a miracle. It's more surprising than your dad dying of septicemia."

I tightened my arm round Guy's shoulders while Joe went to fetch some 'anesthetic'. Guy's expression had changed and reminded me of Claire in one of her worst depressions. I bent and kissed his cheek.

"Go on..." I encouraged.

"I was sitting with Dad three days later - or was it two? I forget. He was cold and very still and was becoming delirious - he kept mentioning the Sisters. His lips had turned blue as if he had frost-bite. He looked up at me, smiled and I actually saw the light go from his eyes."

He gazed up at me again.

"I saw the precise moment of his death, Meg."

He began to sob inconsolably and Joe shoved a glass of whisky in his hand and helped it to his mouth.

"Right!" said Claire brightly. "Let's have something to eat. Come on Margaret - you can give me a hand."

"He can't take any more at the moment - his nerves are shot," my aunt explained, once we were out of hearing. "We need to take a break and do something practical - this'll do as well as anything. How about sausage and mash? Gets the old digestive juices going."

Oh God - she was being so bracing she reminded me of Deidra. I couldn't believe this was the Claire Graham who disappeared into her own mind at the thought of her abusive husband.

When I went to set the table, Joe had taken Guy upstairs and the room was empty, but they re-entered just as Claire brought in the steaming plates of food.

I hadn't thought there was much point in laying a place for our invalid, who came to the table in some of Joe's clothes.

I couldn't have been more wrong. It must have been an age since he'd last had a good hot meal. He polished off the lot in five minutes flat.

Joe got out a pack of cigarettes and leaned back in his chair, blowing smoke out in a steady stream. He pushed the pack and lighter across to Guy who shook his head.

"Martyr," said Joe, and took a drag which lit the end of his cigarette like a sparkler. "Over to you. Want to go on or leave it until morning? I'd take a bet on you not sleeping a wink if you don't get it off your chest.

"Anyway, I'll need to call Kendal for the police tomorrow. Unless you fancy doing this again, you're going to have to let me know what to say."

Guy went back to his armchair by the hearth, while Claire and I returned the crockery to the kitchen.

When we returned, Joe caught his mother's eye. There was real distress in his expression. He motioned for us to sit well removed from the two of them.

"Go on, Guy."

"All I could do for a few days was stand at the bottom of the bed and look at him. He seemed as he always had but somehow smaller and he'd purple bruises across one cheek and down his neck. I'd closed his eyes just after he died but they'd reopened a little as if he was about to wake up."

Guy was beginning to sound unhinged and I was about to tell him to rest for a while when Claire dragged me back by the arm and put her finger to her lips.

"Within a couple of days the body began to smell. I had to do something. I took a mattock and headed down to the bottom of the wheat field thinking the ground would be softer there because of the river, but it was as hard as iron and I couldn't make any impression at all.

"Another day and the stench was unbearable. The only thing I could think of was to put him in the old ice cellar until the ground thawed enough for a proper burial."

This was horrific - he seemed to be totally divorced from what he was saying. How could anyone survive this trauma and retain their sanity?

"I told Mrs. Beattie to wash the place down with disinfectant and scrub the bedding with lye, which she did. It was so cold....so cold.

"I really don't know what happened next. Mrs. Beattie'd been on her way back to the kitchen carrying the sheets to hang over the airer above the fire, When I returned to the house she was laying across the stairs dead as a dodo, the sheets dumped on the hall floor."

He scratched his head, trying to puzzle it out.

"She could have taken a whiff of lye from the sheets if she hadn't rinsed them properly, I suppose. That would have made her dizzy enough to fall. I can't think of anything else, other than she just tripped on the sheets. When

I got back, she was lying as you found her," he said, turning haunted eyes on my cousin.

"Well, that's about it," said Guy, who seemed to have shrunk in on himself.

"How long ago was this?" asked Claire.

"I don't recall," said Guy.

Chapter Thirty-seven

Deidra Does Some Sorting Out

At lunchtime the next day - we didn't get to bed until gone five - I rang Dermot, and Deidra answered.

"Hello there stranger….and what are you wanting this fair morning? Well fair it would be if it didn't have a wind raw as a razors edge. Rob…get your fingers out of that cake mix."

I finally managed to get a word in:

"I need to speak to Dermot."

"He's gone to Kirby for some parts. Will I do?"

"Not unless you can drive a snow plough. I thought Dermot might be able to get a tractor here to get me home. The reason I've been gone so long is we got snowed in and the phone lines've been down at Beckton. It's clearing now but the tractor would've been useful."

"Right - I'll tell 'im," and she put down the phone.

I was gob-smacked when six hours later after the winter darkness had long since fallen, up rolled Deidra on my Massey Ferguson, brandishing a snow shovel like an Amazon warrior.

"Dear God…" said Claire.

"Good Lord." I said.

She'd fetched Paul with her and the poor kid was given the job of digging a path to the door.

"Keep 'im outta mischief," said his mother with satisfaction. "Teach him not to smoke behind the barn."

It was then she caught sight of Guy in the hall. He was still so pale and so troubled everyone was treating him with kid gloves. Not so Deidra.

"What ails thee?" she demanded pushing her way past Claire. "Tha looks like Jacob Marley on a bad day."

We all cringed. Nothing daunted, Deidra pulled the snow shovel from Paul's hands and wrapped Guy's fingers round the handle.

"Bit of exercise'll do thee good. Get shoveling - it'll put roses in yer cheeks."

"Now…" she said to Claire, "get t'kettle on, lass. [1]I'm fair parched. And you needn't think you're getting away wi' anything, Paul O'Connor. There's a spade next to t'door over there. [2]Get thy arse into gear."

By the time Deidra let Paul and Guy back in the house they'd rosy hands as well as cheeks. In the meantime Sarah'd turned up with her mum in tow and both of them were playing sous chef to Deidra's Escoffier in the kitchen. While it was true Deidra had a mouth the size of Morecambe Bay, it was also a fact she had a heart to match.

She dragged me by the arm into the first available empty room which happened to be the preserves pantry.

"What's goin' on 'ere then? There's an atmosphere you

[1]*I'm really thirsty*
[2]*Get going*

could cut wi' a knife." I gave her a condensed version of happenings at Scarsdale. She didn't speak for a full minute.

"Seems to me he needs some 'elp - not coping well by the look of things, is 'e?"

"That would be understating things a bit."

"Can I do anythin'?" she asked.

The thought of Deidra wading into this situation filled me with dread. But then I reconsidered. We'd all been tiptoeing around Guy. Perhaps a dose of Deidra was exactly what he needed. Or perhaps not. Oh well, in for a penny, in for a pound.

"What did you have in mind?"

Straightening out the mess at Scarsdale for a start. Lad needs t' come to terms with happenings at 'is farm and [1]plant 'is dad."

"Please Deidra…please be careful…"

"Don't be daft. I'm not totally witless - managed to charm the WI of Nethershaw, dint I?"

She sorted Guy out in true Deidra style - she threw a tea towel at him and told everyone to leave in colorful language.

"Now, lad. Afore tha says anything else, grab yon cloth and dry these few pots while we fix this little drama o' yorn."

[1]bury his father

167

Guy pulled a chair from under the table and sat down hard.

"I can't - I just can't. It's too much."

[1]"Well, tha'd better get used to it afore Mr. Plod drags thee back for a re-enactment."

"Joe says he'll go."

"'ow does that work? Was 'he there? [1]T'police'll want a blow by blow account. I'll tell thee what - we'll all go first f'moral support. Now get a move on wi' those pots. I sharnt tell thee again."

The following morning that's how Deidra, Claire, Joe, Guy and I ended up at Scarsdale. Paul was left watching football on the TV. Deidra said he'd be fine and would probably take in 'Watch With Mother' too, since he had square eyes.

At Scarsdale Manor Guy occupied himself with the comforting routine of getting hay to the sheep. The rest of us stood looking at each other in dread, afraid of what we were about to find.

."We shouldn't be here," Joe reminded us in a puff of vapor, "Until they've determined otherwise, the police will treat this as a crime scene. We must take care not to disturb anything."

"Sod of it it's snowed then. There'll be footprints all over the shop. Best we pray f'more," muttered Deidra.

[1]*The police'll want to know exactly what happened. We'll all go with you first for moral support. Get a move on with those dishes. I won't tell you again*

"Can't see a problem there," I said glancing at the blackening sky. "Let's get a move on."

Poor old Doris Beattie was still laying as she'd fallen, still stiff as a board if bent in the middle by the stair. Thank God for refrigeration; pity Guy'd kept a fire burning in his dad's room.

The sheets were still lying at the bottom of the stairs in a heap, as they'd fallen when Mrs. Beattie dropped them.

Joe had a quick scout around the other bedrooms but all seemed to be as it should.

Josh's room still had tumbled blankets and rugs knocked askew from his removal, and there were cold grey ashes in the hearth.

Despite Joe's instructions about disturbing things - 'one piler ashes looks much like another' - Deidra cleaned out the kitchen range and lit a blazing fire. When Guy returned, nervous about re-entering, she took him gently by the arm, sat him in the warmth and elected to stay with him.

There were still traces of Mrs. Beattie everywhere - a kettle on the range, flour and eggs laid out on the scrubbed table - even a bowl of frozen milk left down for a long-gone cat. Over all was a faint pall of frost.

Guy knew there was worse to come.

Chapter Thirty-eight

Joe's Dilemma

The worst thing for Guy had been taking Joe to see the whereabouts of his father's body, which he'd hefted into the ice cellar for preservation. He didn't want the ladies present he said - it'd be too much for them. Poor boy had forgotten Claire had shot her husband through the head and Deirdra had no appreciable sensibilities of any description.

We watched from halfway across the yard as Joe opened the trap door with a broom handle, being careful not to leave hand or foot prints. He tried to peer through the underground blackness but gave up. He couldn't climb down for fear of disturbing something.

"Right," said Deidra. [1]"Get yer skates on - time t'go."

They stayed overnight again at Bythwaite and then Deidra set off back on the tractor with Paul perched precariously on the back mudguard.

"Tell Dermot I'll be home in a day or two and to ring if he has any problems," I yelled as she rounded the bend on the lane.

There was still likely to be a mountain of paperwork to discuss with the family lawyer regarding the farm which had now been inherited by Joe. Guy was at Bythwaite to be at hand should the police need him at Scarsdale.

[1]*Hurry - we've to leave now.*

From time to time we found Guy standing in the middle of the lane gazing towards his home, and once as I was taking hay to the sheep, I saw him on the ridge above the Sisters, gazing down at Scarsdale Manor. He wasn't coping well at all.

That *Claire* was worried about *him* was perturbing in itself.

Joe threw his fountain pen down on the desk in his dad's former office - now his own - and blue-black ink flew everywhere.

"Oh SHIT!"

He finally lost his temper.

"Is there no end to it? We sort out one problem and another three rear their heads - it's like a bloody hydra."

"What's wrong?" I asked sympathetically.

"You want me to make a list?" he glared, "Right - I will. I've to try and make head or tail of business tax, employment contracts, accounts, shares, expenses, suppliers, customers, tenants and on top of that there's the lambing season.

"If Guy's too spooked to take over I'll have to find another tenant for Scarsdale. Unless I can figure something out, it's going to be laying fallow with weeds to the window-sills. There'll be no ploughing or muck spreading done for spring planting.

"Then there's business with the holiday lets. We've two available for rent but no-one to handle the business end. Guy did that, but he can hardly drag himself out of bed at the moment."

He stopped short and ran strong fingers through his hair.

"What do I do Meg. I can't face all this - then there's Mum's investment at Ghyll Howe. It's endless."

"We can only start from the beginning and slowly work our way through. Everything will sort itself out in time. Claire and I can help with the paperwork and you can dump all the legal stuff on your solicitor, instructing him to provide you with a report. You'll know how to do a lot of it yourself next time round."

Neither of us had realized Claire was standing in the doorway until she said:

"There's one very good way to deal with Scarsdale if you can persuade Guy to my way of thinking. Why don't you make it over to him?

"In the past few years, you've started up an altogether separate venture. That could be sold off. It's becoming necessary to consolidate. All large businesses have to do that from time to time."

"She's right," I said, "And a while ago you told me I needed to employ a field foreman to free Dermot and helped me with the marketing yourself. We need staff."

"You can count me in."

Guy came in on the end of the discussion and stood quietly behind Claire's shoulder.

"I can't go through life like this. You asked how long I'd been in the house after my father died Mrs. Graham, and I've been thinking about it. I don't think it can have been more than three weeks."

Three weeks - with two dead bodies? It was a wonder he hadn't completely lost his mind.

Claire's face creased in pity, and I put my arms around his waist and hugged him tightly. He gently removed me and stood next to Joe who managed a tight smile.

"What can I do Joe? There must be something."

My cousin looked at his mother and me for confirmation and when we nodded, said:

"How would you feel about going back to Scarsdale?"

Guy looked momentarily panicked.

"But I don't know how that's possible, Joe," said Guy, "It'll always feel like Dad's place. Perhaps it'll be better if I upped sticks and moved to Nethershaw to run the letting agency and help manage Ghyll Howe, if you're still agreeable Meg. Perhaps Mr. Graham's and Dad's deaths have made you see things in a different light?"

Claire waited for Joe to resume.

"You've missed the point, Guy. I'm not talking of you replacing your father. I want to make Scarsdale's deeds over to you. It's yours if you want it."

"Joe can't possibly cope with all this," I said.

"But it's worth thousands - hundreds of thousands! You can't just give it to me!"

"Oh yes he can!" I said wryly. "He's an expert - he gave me double my asking price for Fairview. Granted it wasn't exactly Scarsdale."

"Now, don't be silly Guy," said my aunt tartly, as if he was five years old, "No-one's putting any pressure on you but there is another consideration. All three of you now have substantial assets to carry forward to our new enterprise. We could call it the Graham and Greenwood Agricultural Conglomerate and issue shares."

I couldn't help reflecting on fate:

Maggie Graham of ramshackled Fairview Small-holding near Nethershaw.

Meg Graham of Luneside House, Nethershaw.

Margaret Graham of Ghyll Howe Farm.

What would my title be this time?

As it turned out, it wasn't what I'd expected at all.

Chapter Thirty-nine

The Sisters and Ghyll Howe Again

Joe and Claire were concerned with completing arrangements for the transfer of Bythwaite, so as Dermot was having a fine old time buying tractors and harvesters and Deidra was now terrorizing the WI in Nethershaw, I decided to make myself useful and offered to help Guy make Scarsdale his own, and not just a memory of his dad. After all, I'd had plenty of experience - I'd started off doing up two rooms at Ghyll Howe and ended up stripping it, replastering and redecorating most of it.

Half way through the afternoon I went looking for Guy. He wasn't in the farm buildings or the house and eventually I found him sitting in the Stone Circle. I had the very odd notion the Sisters were protecting him.

He was gazing towards the brow of the hill from where he could have seen Scarsdale Manor Farm spread below.

"Come - let's take a look." I said quietly, careful not to startle him.

"I was just wondering if I could," he said.

I took his hand, helped him to his feet and together we walked the few steps to the hill top.

A few uniformed policemen moved purposefully across the yard far below, packing things into the back of a van under the direction of someone in overalls.

Good... it looked as if they were leaving.

"I'd thought in a little while when you feel stronger, we might redecorate - maybe update Scarsdale. I would be happy…."

Witch Stones

His head snapped up and for a split second he looked at me suspiciously. Then I was shocked into silence when he dragged me to him and kissed me hard on the lips.

After a pretty enjoyable few seconds, we sprang apart and regarded each other with surprise.

"I'm sorry," he muttered and turned to leave.

"The hell you are!" I said, grabbing him and returning the favor.

It was so good I had the distinct feeling the stones behind us were smiling.

He dragged me back down the slope and propped me against one of the stones. Again I felt the subtle vibration. It was intoxicating. The proper kissing began and went on for several minutes, until we both got hot and bothered. As soon as I moved from the stone the pulsing stopped.

By silent agreement we headed back down the hill to Bythwaite before things got completely out of hand.

"Oh I'm so pleased!" said Claire, without prompting. "It's certainly about time. You've been pussy-footing round each other for months."

For my own part, I was doubtful it'd amount to much. Guy was in desperate need of comfort and I'd been there at the right time, that was all. God knows what *he* thought. I began to feel embarrassed and blushed. He put his arms around me and rubbed his lips across my hot cheek.

"No need," he whispered in my ear. "It's true."

When we looked, Claire had gone.

Witch Stones

This was a new situation for me - pleasurable, yes, but confusing. Fortunately his bashfulness put Guy in the same boat. No doubt we'd work things out between us but perhaps it was fortunate we were in the middle of a very busy time.

I could no longer avoid going home. Although Dermot was proving to be an efficient manager, I seemed to have abandoned him. On further thought, it occurred to me he'd probably be happier at that moment playing with his new tractors and harvester and hiring staff. He probably hadn't even noticed I wasn't there.

I expected to get an earful from Deidra who missed my company between bouts at the chapel, where I understood she was knocking the new minister into shape.

Joe would be occupied at Bythwaite for some considerable time to come.

Now the coppers had removed themselves, and the bodies of Josh and Mrs. Beattie from Scarsdale, Guy had steeled himself to return to his home.

He rang me to say not to rush back - he'd never seen the place as the police had left it in the whole of his life. It was pristine inside and out.

Once Claire had finished with the paperwork for Joe, and getting her own home as she wanted it, she came over to Ghyll Howe with a whole sheaf of documents regarding our new venture. I signed on the dotted line… a lot, but asked Claire not to push forward with anything until Joe and Guy were ready, and I'd made sure everything was okay at my end. I was beginning to see total strangers wandering about my yard, which was disconcerting until Dermot lined them up to be introduced.

There were eight new ones whereas I'd expected six as discussed. All were lads I recognized from the town. One was Tom Braithwaite who'd pulled my hair and told me I looked 'a scrow' when I first came down from the fells to work at Luneside. I couldn't find it in me to bear a grudge. Time had marched on.

Joe was snowed under, so it was time to make a personal visit to my customers - they had been pretty much abandoned over the months since Dick had died and we'd been snowed in. It took me three days and I'd only lost two of them, which was great news.

Dermot had seen to the preparation of my land for planting which was still a few weeks off, so I decided to go and help Guy sort out his home before his own year's work began.

[1]"Get yon lad sorted and never mind the hanky-panky," *had everyone known but me?* "We'll be needing you back here for t'planting, come t'beginning' o' t'month," said Deidra, and clipped Rob round the ear when he added:

"Aye, right enough."

My Lord that boy was a good-looker with his wild chestnut curls, tanned skin and deep brown eyes,. He'd grown a foot since last I'd seen him and he was going to drive the local girls wild.

[1]*Get that boy of yours sorted out and never mind the fooling around.... We'll be needing you back at Ghyll Howe for the planting at the beginning of the month.*

Now Ghyll Howe was sorted to my satisfaction, it was time to fulfil my promise to Guy and help get him back on track.

Chapter Forty

Business Concluded and Unexpected Violence

Guy had decided to lay his father to rest in the place he had first thought of, in sight of the river and overhung with willow. Josh would prefer it there rather than the churchyard he said, as his father's religion was closer to the fruitful earth than the pulpit.

Claire said:

"Quite right too. Josh brought Guy to manhood close to The Seven Sisters. It's only right he should feel their power himself."

As I pulled through the gate of Scarsdale Manor, Guy was standing in the middle of the yard, turning about and taking in the farm as if for the first time.

That wasn't surprising. He'd never had anything entirely his own - even his car had belonged to Uncle Dick.

"Come on then," I began cheerily, banging shut my car door. "It's not about to fix itself. You'd better ring some of those lads of yours to help."

He turned and his entire expression changed. Suddenly, he was full of confidence and exhilaration for what the future held.

With the aid of a few of the farm lads, happy their jobs looked to be safe, we made short work of stripping the whole house to the plaster and repainting inside and out….. after I'd got those bloody windows replaced. Frost should stay on the outside.

A few days later, I watched a cement mixer roll dripping into the yard. The driver filled in the hole where the icehouse had been, and Joe suggested Guy should complete the job by hiring a man with a pneumatic drill to get rid of the rest of the ruined building.

That evening Claire, Joe, Guy and I took a little time out of our busy schedule to relax in the 'Pick and Shovel' in Beckton. Much to the landlord's delight, Claire bought a magnum of Champagne and shared it among his clientele. We drank to new beginnings.

At closing time, Joe grinned knowingly at Claire as Guy remarked on the beauty of the starry night and suggested he and I walk back to Bythwaite rather than riding in Claire's car. True it was starry, but that was only because the air was bitter.

Nevertheless I began to realize more and more that Guy was absolutely my type: backwards in coming forwards whereas I was pushy; considerate where I usually opened my mouth without a thought for the outcome, and so handsome - tall and strong, blue-eyed and with unruly fair hair, whereas I still looked like Peter Pan - marginally less than flat as a pancake. What *did* he see in me?

In the history of finance I'd like to bet a business venture never came together so fast. The gist was that the holiday lets were bought up by a local consortium; Joe and Guy would work their respective farms, and Claire and I would manage the finances together with the solicitor, until we could find a better solution.

It was also decided Claire, Joe and I would remain at Bythwaite, and Guy would go back to Scarsdale once it was in a habitable condition. It worked out very well, although I don't think me being in Bythwaite while he was in Scarsdale appealed to Guy at all.

The years went by and the people changed with the turning of the seasons.

Paul and Sean were now grown and were becoming very committed farmers. Paul had quit University much to Deidra's fury, when he discovered he shared his father and brother's love of the soil. The boys were very different. Sean was like his father and never happier than when covered in mud. Paul was a businessman by nature and became very much Joe's protégé.

"Little" Robbie had become a bean-stalk with a smile to melt granite, and a gaggle of giggly girls following in his wake like ducklings. Deidra kept a very close eye on him but he was becoming better at eluding her and there was an awful lot of tittering from behind the barn on WI nights.

Guy had lost the edge off his shyness over the months and become everything I could have wanted - kind, strong of arm and character, charming and my absolute soul-mate. Our love blossomed and deepened as the months passed.

"Joined at the hip," said Deidra fondly - although he was at Scarsdale and I at Ghyll Howe.

Guy had 'moth-balled' his office in Nethershaw in case it should be needed, but we'd outgrown it and it had no purpose, so he put the lease back in the hands of the estate agent.

Claire was spending a few days at Ghyll Howe. On an unseasonably warm Spring day I packed up chicken sandwiches and a rhubarb tart and we headed down to the river.

Just as I was about to spread the picnic cloth beside a heaven-scented elderflower tree, Claire shouted out in pain. When I turned it was to see Valerie Mitford-Clarke swinging her round by the hair. She looked wild, and half-way to losing her mind.

Claire was too busy trying to free her hair to take much notice of what she was saying.

"Thought I'd forgotten? I'll bet you did!" she snarled. "The past always catches up with the likes of you, Claire Graham!"

"Val! Let go at once. Let go, I said."

A man's voice shouted across the field behind us, and I became aware of Peter Mitford-Clarke pelting across the field as fast as his middle-aged legs would carry him. This was the first I'd seen of him since he'd been marched off down the court steps by two burly policemen.

Peter fetched his wife a whack across the face, which simultaneously made her eyes water and drop Claire's hair. Nevertheless, she continued to glare at us. If I'd done something, I was buggered if I knew what. This was on a par with the bombing of Hiroshima to me.

"Ask her!" yelled Valerie, in fury. "Ask her!"

Claire had by now regained her composure, tidied her hair and straightened her shoulders.

"I apologize for my wife's terrible behavior," said Peter. "I hope you will forgive us. Come on Valerie - it's time we went home. I'm so sorry Meg, I don't know what happened but she saw you and Mrs. Graham from the road and leapt from the car. It's a wonder she wasn't killed."

"Take her away, Mr. Mitford-Clarke. It's about time Margaret knew what went on anyway. Take her away."

"And when she's finished spinning you a pack of lies," growled Valerie, "you can come and ask my side of the story because you can bet your life it'll be nothing like hers."

This was only the second time Valerie had seen Claire and I together I realized, and both times had been nasty.

Chapter Forty-one
Claire's Shocking Revelation

They left, Peter holding his wife tightly by the wrist.

The glade we were sitting in became unnaturally quiet. We were both momentarily bereft of speech and the bird-life, with the exception of a solitary song thrush high in a nearby tree, was probably winging its way to the safety of the Seven Sisters by then.

"What do you know about your mother and father?" Claire asked quietly.

I thought about it hard. What did I know? I knew my dad grew up at Bythwaite, his family home, with his brother Richard and parents Mary or Molly Carrick and Joseph Graham, and the last only because I came across an old photograph; I knew somehow my dad and his brother fell out and Robert brought his own family up in a ruin on Aidafell near Nethershaw.

I knew both my uncle and father were sheep farmers and that they married sisters Claire and Moira Armstrong from Manchester.

Anything else was supposition. It seemed to me my father was held in some affection locally and certainly by Claire, but that his brother seemed to hate him like the devil and had driven him away. I had been told that Robert was the apple of his mother's eye.

And then there had been Valerie Mitford-Clarke's amazing reaction to Claire. What was that about?

"I know virtually nothing, but I've never thought about it before" I said, my brow furrowed, "My dad was never there. Ellen was older but I pretty much brought Johnny up on my own. Mother died of the pneumonia not long after Johnny was born. I don't remember her clearly - only that she had curly hair and read me bedtime stories from an old book with Red Riding Hood on the cover."

I saw Claire's eyes had filled with tears.

"I loved Moira so much and I did her so much harm. But if we had our time over again, I don't know if I would have done anything different. You see, I loved him beyond reason."

"Who?"

There was a long pause during which Claire skimmed a flat pebble uselessly over the river.

"Robert."

"MY DAD?"

The tears began to course down her cheeks.

"Yes, God forgive me."

Well, that put a stopper in my mouth. My brain totally shut down. When I could finally find the words, I asked:

"I don't mean to be disrespectful, Claire….. but weren't you married at the time?"

"Yes - we both were. Moira married Robert, then I married Richard a couple of years later. I'd always held Robert in great affection, but the day I married Richard our eyes met over the table at the reception, and our fates were sealed. The realization we could do nothing about it mortified us both. I saw Moira tug at his arm and for a moment he couldn't turn away."

"Oh, God! Is there more?"

"That's the tip of the iceberg. Do you hate me?"

I was filled with such pity for her I just hugged her, stroking her hair.

"You might not feel so sympathetic once you find out what happened later."

Claire had fallen in love with her sister's husband on her own wedding day. Surely it couldn't get any worse.

She drew her knees up and rested the side of her head on them, examining me closely. I could see she was distraught and her face began to take on the familiar vacant expression.

"Get a hold of yourself aunt, or I'll be obliged to fetched Deidra."

That snapped her back to herself. A beating by Mrs. O'Connor was one thing, but two quite another.

"Yes darling," she said hurriedly, "you're right. We wouldn't like to disturb Deidra. She was so good to me last time."

The hell she was!

"I won't press you now Claire, just as long as you realize you have to give me the whole story because if you don't, Valerie will."

"Valerie's maiden name was Elliot, by the way," she added mysteriously as we packed away the picnic.

Witch Stones

How long before Claire was in any fit condition to tell me why Valerie had the same surname as the bloke whose body was stuffed in my water butt - or two maiden ladies who ran the Methodist Sunday School in Nethershaw?

Chapter Forty-two

Dermot and Deidra Promoted

Claire drove back home the following day, I dare say with a fair bit of relief to be gone. She whipped off down the road in Joe's Healey, nearly taking the gate post with her bumper.

I stayed another month to help supervise the last of the planting and go over the accountant's report on the year-end tax returns with Dermot. I needed to look out a couple of office staff for him. Although he tried to do it all himself, that wasn't possible even though eighteen year old Sean, who had inherited his mother's forthright nature, was shaping up to be a pretty good foreman. Paul, as trainee salesman thanks to Joe, was unfazed by the 'nobs from down south'.

Now she'd come round to the idea that whatever her opinion, her lads were going to be farmers, Deidra had given in. She'd come to the same conclusion I had about Dermot's job, and her husband and two sons in well-paid employment was not to be sneezed at.

The lads Dermot had taken on, had turned out well, and he'd supplemented them with a few of the older local school kids at weekends, through busy times of year.

There seemed to be a small army pulling cap brims and saying 'mum' in deference as I collected my mug of tea from Deidra, who had continued her self-appointed job of cooking and cleaning. She'd taken on one of the Misses Elliot as second in command, and some of the older girls from the village whose parents couldn't afford to keep them on at school.

I had come to rely on Deidra's good sense so much. That, and the clean home and dinner I always came back to. We'd slipped into something of a sisterly relationship. The only thing which interfered was my holding the purse-strings. Not that that was too much of a problem since she seemed to be able to get me to whop up Dermot's wages at will.

She'd taken on so much on a voluntary basis, I gave her a pay packet of her own, and 'petty cash' to run the kitchen which I had extended and fitted out for her.

Robbie was still at the Grammar School and running rings round the local girls at the Saturday Night Hop at the Village Hall. Gone were the chestnut curls, now molded with Brylcreem into a DA Elvis would've been proud of, but the soft brown eyes remained his trademark.

"That kid'll get himself into bother," said Deidra to me, chewing her lip as she watched Rob walk off down the lane in his leather jacket, the collar turned up and a pair of skin tight jeans which showed off his apple-cheek bum to perfection. I could see what she meant.

"Oh, well," she sighed. "At least he won't be a bloody farmer.

"Right," I said to Dermot. "You should be just about straight. Let me know if you want to interview senior staff, and I'll be back. For now I'm off to Scarsdale. Don't let Deidra anywhere near potential office workers."

Witch Stones

"Surprised you've managed to pry yourself away from yon lad for this long," he said with a grin. "He'll be getting' fair randy by now. Watch thi-sel," and he returned to his office chortling.

I glared after him, then returned to my car, admitting he was probably right. Claire could wait another twenty-four hours.

Despite the smell of manure, there's something ethereal about a farm in Spring.

Before the first freshness appears on the trees and in the fields, there is a sense of growing things, living things pushing their way through the earth. Then one by one daffodils and crocuses unfurl, and shy little primroses and forget-me-nots spring from skirts of vivid green. The riverbanks are profuse with wood anemones and wild garlic - or 'onion stinks' as Deidra called them unromantically but with good reason.

Living things, babies - tadpoles becoming frogs, fox cubs somersaulting and growling between ancient tree roots, song thrushes shouting their beautiful warnings from the tree tops.

I think it must have been a female thing, because Guy and Joe never seemed to notice, and if I mentioned it Guy looked at me as if I was crazy. They needed to lift their heads and take in their surroundings.

That was how it was on the sunny April day I pulled into the yard at Scarsdale Manor Farm.

Guy hadn't known when to expect me so wasn't at the house when I arrived.

A girl in her early twenties hurried through the kitchen door and stopped short in surprise. It was a moment or two before I realized it was the very same girl who had served us tea in cracked mugs the day I first met Josh Greenwood.

She'd come on a bit since then. Golden curls were tied up from her face in a ponytail, and whisps had escaped prettily to frame her smooth face. He would either fire her voluntarily or under duress. Either way she was going.

"Hello, Miss Graham. Grand to see thee again after all this time. Come and sit while I make some tea. You'll happen not remember me - I'm Carol, Carol Williamson what used to work for poor Mr. Josh."

With true Sarah familiarity she continued:

"Guy'll be back directly. There's some late lambs up near t'Sisters."

She twittered on. Apparently, Guy had offered her her old job back a couple of weeks before, and she'd been pleased to accept.

Aye, I bet she was!

There was a clatter at the door and a voice shouted:

"Last ewe's just dropped on the top field. That's one job out of the way. It's a relief, I was beginning....."

He saw me, and his face wreathed in smiles he said:

"Meg, Meggie my darling!" and he picked me up and danced me round the room, peppering my face with kisses.

Then he stopped and his kisses and breathing deepened. Much against my will, I realized I'd have to stop this before we ended up on the hearth rug in front of Carol. I suddenly felt smug and a lot more confident.

Unfortunately, Carol had disappeared in time to miss the extent of his ardor.

"Carol," he yelled. "put a picnic basket together. We're going down to the mill."

In his stocking feet he made my tea.

Chapter Forty-three

An Unexpected Proposal

We walked across the self-same fields we'd travelled the first time I'd visited Scarsdale, when the workers had been harvesting hay and the scent was overpoweringly sweet.

But this was growing time and the meadows were filled with burgeoning poppies and cornflowers, daisies and wild scabious, bright as jewels. I had everything I'd ever dreamed of and the sun was shining brightly.

Guy must have felt the same, because he strode along the grassy path whistling and swinging the picnic basket, until I feared for the condition of our lunch.

He had already thought out a spot to eat. He spread a cloth and handed me down to sit on a banking of pincushion moss, as if I was Cinderella and he Prince Charming.

Something was going on - I could feel it but couldn't figure out why he was so jumpy.

At the end of our meal he recited:

> *Goldilocks Goldilocks wilt thou be mine?*
>
> *Thou shalt not do the dishes nor yet feed the swine,*
>
> *But sit on a cushion and sew a fine seam,*
>
> *And feed upon strawberries, sugar and cream.*

I dug him in the ribs and laughed. He reached into his pocket and flipped open a tiny box decorated with a silk rosette. Inside was a ring the like of which I'd never seen. The central stone was a large square sapphire. Cushion-cut, it was supported on either side by two baguette diamonds. It was as brilliantly beautiful as the flowers we sat amongst.

"Well?"

"If you think I'm mending holes in your bloody shirts Guy Greenwood, you've got another thing coming. Dermot and I have to ready the eight acre field for planting," I said blushing furiously.

"For once in your life Margaret Graham, will you forget the root veg and think of the swain who's doing his best to court you?"

All those girls who had passed him by because of his shyness, had missed the biggest prize of all. We made our plans and drew explosive passion from touch and the fecund earth.

"The jeweler says we can change it if you don't like it," he said against my lips.

That was the enchantment of a Spring proposal. We were both starry-eyed - probably sickeningly so for most people, but unfortunately I'd to go to Bythwaite to tackle Claire about the mystery of the bloody Elliots.

Guy drove me to Bythwaite. He kept looking at me and sweetly kissing my cheek, which was all very well but he was driving down a lane five yards wide with no passing places. Still, he seemed to know what he was doing as we didn't end up in a ditch.

"Oh please let me see it!" said Claire clutching her hands together in delight.

"See what?" said Joe.

"The ring of course. When two people show up at your door with witless expressions and leaves in their hair, either they're due for a padded cell or they just got engaged!"

"Oh, is that all?" said Joe going back to his newspaper. "That's been coming on for months."

We went through the usual 'oos and ahs' from Claire, who adored the ring, and were pointedly ignored by my cousin, who clearly hadn't a romantic bone in his body.

When Guy and Joe began talking fat stock and abattoirs, I decided this would be as good a time as any to tackle Claire.

"Sarah - fetch us tea and cake to my garden please."

"Who is she this week?" I asked with a grin.

"Sandra Dee - we've graduated from singers to actresses."

Sarah's entertainment value would be the envy of those she idolized

.

Chapter Forty-four

A Wedding and a Honeymoon

When we returned to the sitting room, the subject matter had roamed to infected pasturage and foot-rot.

Claire floated in purposefully, sat on the sofa between her son and his friend, and pointedly began a conversation with me on the merits of various flours in the preparation of Yorkshire pudding.

Even Joe got the message, so Claire moved to an easy chair and I sat next to my beloved and smiled up into his face. The poor soul blushed furiously.

"Oh really, Guy. You can't stand at the altar like that - your face will clash with the bridesmaids' dresses. I'm considering primrose-yellow with a seed-pearl trim - and long gloves. What do you think, Margaret?" said Claire.

How on earth had she managed to get to that point of view so quickly? I'd only just sat down.

Later, I was leaning against a drystone wall, while Guy chewed on a blade of grass, and gazed thoughtfully at sheep peacefully grazing in the adjoining field.

"Where shall we go for a honeymoon?" I asked. "You've lambing and shearing out of the way. If I kicked Claire in the backside she could have everything sorted within the month."

"Hadn't really thought about it," he said.

Of course he hadn't, and neither had anyone else except Claire.

She took over the wedding planning like a sergeant major - even the vicar looked terrified.

It was typical C of E - flowers everywhere, even tied to the end of the pews, mostly white chrysanths - they didn't drop said auntie - and pink and peach roses with lots of green stuff to fill them out. I marched down the aisle to Mendelssohn - dah dah de dah. Claire and Deidra were Maids of Honor since both were long past the 'brides-maid' stage, and Sean, Paul and Robbie - DA and winkle-pickers looking ridiculous with his morning suit and tie stud - were groomsmen. Joe of course was Best Man, and infinitely more composed than the groom, who periodi-cally he appeared to be holding upright.

I naturally looked gorgeous. Auntie had outdone herself. I'd a coronet of blush roses and cream fresia, and a dress spud planters dream about. It took me a full hour to scrub the soil ingrained under my nails but I finally managed it, and Claire painted them with clear polish.

Carol Williamson, Guy's temporary housekeeper, sniffed loudly into a hankie throughout the service, and 'Marilyn' Lumb, the Beckton 'wiggle', gazed hopefully at Joe.

I did wonder about my brother Johnnie and sister Ellen - vaguely.

Despite being able to afford to visit my sister in Bermuda, Guy and I spent a week in Blackpool on our honeymoon. I don't remember the place at all except it had a prom, a beach and a tower. We seemed to spend most of our time 'resting' in our hotel room or gazing ridiculously at each other over ice-cream cones.

Witch Stones

God, I loved him! He was so handsome and managed to be both shy and a whiz in bed. What a combination!

The one conversation of note we did have was about where we'd make our permanent home. Joe may have given Scarsdale Manor Farm to Guy when his father died, but I still had Ghyll Howe to run and that was miles away, as Dermot had so colorfully pointed out. We chewed it over but by the end of our time away we'd come to no solution.

We returned to Scarsdale still perplexed and not a little worried.

Claire had already taken charge of our home because the place shone like a new pin. There was a casserole in the oven and a table set for two with a candle on it.

Joe, who had been managing the farm while we were away, was just on the point of pulling out of the yard as we arrived, so we asked him to eat with us before he left.

As I found some more cutlery in a drawer and dished up the food, Guy was explaining our problem. Joe came up with the answer before Guy had finished his first sentence:

"Great holiday, I take it," said Joe with a wink. Guy turned pink and ignored the understatement.

"Aye. It would have been if we hadn't spent so much time discussing where......"

"And you didn't think to hand Ghyll Howe over to Dermot as tenant? What were you thinking? Oh, don't answer that!"

Witch Stones

"I've lived on a tenant farm all my life and it never occurred. I was thinking whether to lay the wheat field fallow next season."

Joe spluttered.

"Is that a fact?"

"Shut up Joe." I said, then looked at them both angrily.

"When you've both finished carving up my farm, I'd like to put in my two [1]pen'th. I built that farm from scratch by the sweat of my own brow - which neither of you can claim."

I thought of Deidra who would become kingpin at the WI if I became mistress of Scarsdale. Wouldn't she just love lording it over the likes of Mrs. Wilson and her macramé?

"Depending on Dermot's reaction, I'm in," I said quietly. "Break out the bubbly!"

[2]Tetley's was the next best thing.

[1]*have my own say*
[2]*brand of beer*

Chapter Forty-five

Independence for Dermot O'Connor

I was in the kitchen [1]chewing the fat with Deidra when Dermot came in from the fields for his tea.

"Get the fuck out of here you bastard. There's more muck on them boots than a peat bog. Leave 'em outside on't scraper."

When he walked back in in stocking feet, I said:

"I'd like you to please sit down. I have something important to discuss with you."

"What's the [2]meat-'ed done now?" Deidra asked looking suspiciously at her husband.

Dermot looked baffled.

"No nothing like that," I replied testily. "For once in your life shut up Deidra and let somebody else get a word in."

"I will if y'promise not t'sack 'im!"

Paul chortled. His mother batted him round the ear.

I paused. How did I tackle this? It would be an incredible change for the whole family; could they cope with it? Did Dermot have sufficient skills? Well he seemed to have survived pretty well so far.

I took a deep breath and continued:

"This isn't a firm offer you underst....."

"We can't do wi' more work now, Meg - err, sorry Mrs.

[1]*gossiping*
[2]*meat-head - fool*

Greenwood. It'll break the camel's back."

The kettle whistle blew unattended until Deidra kicked Paul on the shins.

"Keep [1]yer kecks on - I was just…."

"SHUT UP!"

Finally she got the message. I turned to Dermot who was twiddling his thumbs waiting for the furore to subside.

"Mr. Graham, Mr. Greenwood and I wondered how you would feel about taking on Ghyll Howe as tenant."

I let out a breath and became aware of the loud tick of the Victorian wall-clock behind me. The silence was deafening and went on for long enough to make me uneasy.

Deidra opened a drawer and pulled out a pack of cigarettes and some kitchen matches. When did she begin smoking?

"My God, Meg - oh, can't do the Mrs. Greenwood bit now - you don't mess around, do you? Here - 'ave a [2]fag!"

I shook my head - I felt sick enough already.

"Well, Dermot - what do you think?"

But he'd already left.

I found him fixing a hole in a fence.

"I take it that's a 'no'," I said.

He was weeping with emotion. I'd never seen a fifty

[1]*calm down*
[2]*cigarette*

something-year-old-man cry before, except Peter Mitford-Clarke when he was frightened he'd been found out. That was quite a different situation.

"Oh Missus…Miss Graham," he reddened, and his mouth opened and closed like a goldfish. "Sorry… Mrs. Greenwood, Ma'am."

"Good grief, Dermot - what on earth's wrong with you? I haven't recommended you for [1]the Honors List."

"My own… my own farm. Oh…. Mrs. Greenwood."

"Well, technically it'd still be ours, but it'd be yours to run as you see fit so long as you turn a profit. There's the chance of you becoming a stakeholder too, but you'll need to discuss that with Mr. Graham."

He jogged off down the lane, too full of emotion to speak.

[1]*At New Year, the Monarch presents titles for services to the nation.*

Chapter Forty-six

Sex and The Sisters

I was told by Deidra in no uncertain terms, Dermot would be accepting my offer. Poor man - between me and his wife he didn't stand a cat in hells, but I don't think he cared. He spent the three days until Claire, Joe and Guy turned up, whistling tunelessly and grinning to himself.

I left the three men to work out the business end of his employment and drove Claire for a spot of lunch at the Lion. I wanted to hear more about my dad.

Once she'd made herself comfortable in a well-worn bow-back chair, and was half way down her gin and tonic, I said:

"Well?"

"Well what, Margaret dear?"

This was like [1]drawing teeth.

"What about the Grahams, Armstrongs and Elliots? What did you think I meant?"

"From what I said before, you'll appreciate things were touchy in the Graham-Armstrong camp. Richard's father had died just after we married, and Richard being the elder, once he'd taken control of the farm, kicked Robert out.

"Robert took Moira, already pregnant with your sister, to Nethershaw, where he worked as a farm laborer until my sister's time drew near. He'd borrowed enough money to buy the lease on Fairview and a few animals to make a

[1]hard work

beginning. His mother bought the freehold for him against Richard's express instructions. When he found out he threatened to put her out of the house.

"Nothing happened for a while. None of us saw each other."

A tear rolled down her cheek.

I went back to the bar to replenish our glasses and give her time to

compose herself. When I returned, she grabbed my arm as I sat, and said earnestly:

"Please forgive me, Margaret but you must understand - I had deep love for your father, but there was also over-whelming lust which fills me with shame."

It's not often an aunt confides such details to her niece, particularly about her own father.. I must have looked floored because she said:

"We'll stop there if you like. I must have shocked you but I have never before spoken of this to a soul. It's such a relief to unload my grief - and my devastating guilt."

"I'd rather you went on, Claire. For the time being at least," I said, nervously.

"Robert and I used to meet up at the Seven Sisters. In the dead of night it's so ghostly that people avoid it. I don't know why the stones buzz - you mentioned feeling it yourself when you kissed Guy. Robert and I felt it too.

"Over time, one or two visits turned into a regular weekly event. I loved and hated it in equal measure. I loved it because of how I felt for your father, and hated what it must do to Moira if she ever found out. I certainly would have remade my life with Robert if not for her."

"Did you feel no remorse for your husband?"

She looked at me as if I'd lost my mind.

"I put a bullet through his brain - what do you think?

"Our lives continued like this for a couple of years, getting more and more fraught with the passage of time."

There was a longer pause and her brow creased in pain.

"You were born and Moira was so happy. She loved her babies so much.

"By this time Robert and I had thrown all caution to the winds. Our affair had been going on for a couple of years and I suppose we just got lazy. One night Josh Greenwood caught us when he'd gone to check his father's animals. He must have stood watching for a few minutes and when he stepped out from behind one of the stones, I grabbed my clothes and ran. He had been very close to Robert from childhood - he never said a word to a soul.

"When you were three years old and John was a newborn, my sister died of pneumonia and was buried at Nethershaw."

Claire was crying openly by now and beginning to attract attention. I looked around surreptitiously and passed a hankie under the table. She rubbed her eyes and blew her nose loudly as if she had a cold.

"I'm sure you can imagine what happened next. We threw discretion to the winds. We could be alone in a remote croft on the moors."

She stopped suddenly. Joe and Guy had arrived at our table carrying glasses of beer and gin.

"Hello girls," said Joe, then with concern, "You're alright Mum - not sickening for anything, I hope? We've some legal work to discuss."

Chapter Forty-seven

Unbreakable Vows

Claire *was* sick the following day but it had nothing to do with a cold.

She'd slipped back into her absent state and I put her to bed. It would be some time before I dared broach the subject of my mother and father with her while she was in such a delicate state. And I still didn't know why Matt Elliot had ended up in my water barrel, or who the hell Valerie Elliot and Hugo Peter Mitford-Clarke were.

Joe was concerned, but knew he could leave her safely with me, confident I'd get her back on track. It had been years since her last attack.

Joe left the following morning for Beckton, having put the contracts on hold until his mother was on top of her game again.

Guy was another matter - I couldn't lie to him to save my life, so I told him everything - as I knew it so far, pointing out I didn't have the full story.

Just when I thought I was going to need to call Deidra, Claire roused herself and although they were still dimmed with pain, I saw the light return to her eyes.

"Margaret… Meg," she reached desperately for my arm and grasped it tightly. "I swear to you, whatever happens I will never - NEVER - involve you in this awful mess again. It's just that… I became so terrified of Richard over the years, that recounting our story frightened the life out of me. I am so, so sorry. Well, he's not here anymore. I have to remember that.

"I'm getting up now. Please don't tell Deidra," Claire pleaded.

For a moment she looked genuinely terrified.

Guy was with Dermot. Under the pretext of examining the crop, he'd gone to grill him on his real thoughts for his future and particularly his fears.

As Deidra sat down in my kitchen with a nervous Claire, and reheated chicken and veg soup, she said:

[1]"Sit down lass. I can get nowt from this'un so I'll 'ave chapter and verse from thee. It'll give thee practice at not having a relapse."

Irish? The only thing Irish about her now was her name.

"Do I have to? I'm so tired."

"Get on with it. I 'aven't got all day."

Deidra got a shortened version of the conversation in the pub, although at times I did wonder what goddam business it was of hers.

I began to pay attention when we got to what I'd yet to learn.

We ate soup, the clock ticked. One of the lads yelled profanities from outside. Claire continued:

[1]*Sit down my girl. I can't get anything out of this one, so I'll have the whole story from you. It'll give you practice at not having another relapse.*

"When I conceived - as of course was inevitable, Richard refused to speak to me for the entire time of my confinement. He had that dreadful room decorated and furnished and built a wall round a bit of the garden. There Joe was born."

There was a protracted silence.

"Bloody hell! Joe's Meg's BROTHER?" said Deidra who was always quick on the uptake.

Claire looked mortified by her confession.

"Yes - half-brother. Joe was Robert's, but I was his mother. Richard would have nothing to do with either of us until it dawned on him the chances of us having our own children were absolutely zero - we'd had no physical relationship in a long time.

"Then his attitude changed. Joe was his only chance of holding on to

Bythwaite as he got older. It broke my heart to see how Joseph was used and how terrified he became.

"I was never let out again. Not seeing Robert was agony and my imprisonment well-nigh unbearable. I gradually began to fail and my grasp on reality lessened as time went on, until you rescued me my darling Meg. You saved my life enough for me to help Joe. Swapping an incarceration for a jail sentence would have meant very little if Joe found freedom. That's the other reason I put Richard where he deserved to be.

"Please…. promise me neither of you will ever, ever tell a soul about this. No-one knew but Richard, Robert and I and an elderly servant who was the only one allowed near me. She died years ago, and now Richard and Robert are gone, I'm the only one who knows the full truth. That I've entrusted to you but Joe must never know."

She was thoughtful for a moment, then looked momentarily panic-stricken.

"There's one other person who knows. But her reputation would suffer if she opened her mouth. I think I can be reasonably sure of her silence. I'll tell you about her in due course."

"You do realize at some point I'm going to have to tell Guy, don't you, Claire?"

[1]"Well, hell'll freeze over afore Dermot gets a word out of me. Newlyweds're allus full o' this shit. You have my word on it."

[1]*hell will freeze over before Dermot gets a word out of me.*

Chapter Forty-eight

Valerie's Shattering Discovery

A few weeks later, Claire and I were walking along the riverside path near the old mill at Scarsdale. She was humming to herself and collecting oxeye daisies growing beneath the trees.

"What about the Elliots, Claire. Where do they come into all this?" I asked.

She sighed as she arranged the flowers into a neater bunch.

"This is the worst bit of all, because we'd been responsible for our own downfall, and she was caught in the crossfire."

"You remember me saying there was another who knew these secrets? It was Valerie Elliot. She was a pretty young thing - practical, sensible for her age.

"After Moira died, Valerie used to struggle up to Fairview with food and clothing for you children until Robert could cope. Johnny couldn't stay there - he was still a baby and needed constant attention. She took him home with her and cared for him until his father could cope. Her mother who was a devout Methodist was furious, but against her better judgement gave in when Valerie reminded her of her Christian duty.

"As no-one in Nethershaw knew where the baby had come from but had seen her carrying him up and down the fell to Fairview, the gossips began to fill in the gaps with imagination, and the news was whispered that John was Valerie's love-child and Robert his father.

Witch Stones

"The day Valerie returned Johnny to Fairview for the last time before she was sent off to school in Carlisle and out of the way of wagging tongues, she caught us. She held the baby in her arms and looked at us lying there on Moira's bed, naked and breathless and was thunderstruck. She laid John on the bed and fled.

"Matthew Elliot was her cousin and Ruth and Marjorie her aunts - her dead father's sisters.

"Despite Valerie's insistence, Matthew was convinced by the evil tongues of the town, that John was her son and he was being spun a tissue of lies to cover up the facts. He lay in wait and watched her repeatedly take John to Fairview and return with him a couple of hours later, giving credence to the tale-tellers' lies."

Claire shivered, got up and walked along the bank for a few yards, a rising wind pulling at her hair.

"Let's go," I said. "It's a long distressing story. Another day will do."

We crossed the pack bridge in silence. As we walked, I wondered how Matt, the relaxed and contented man of the earth I'd come to know, had once been the heartless bully of Claire's description.

As she got in her car to go home, she said:

"Will you come with me to Ghyll Howe tomorrow? Perhaps the drive would do us both good."

Over our evening meal, I told Guy I'd be going over to Ghyll Howe the following day with Claire. She had some papers for Dermot to sign, and phone numbers to pass on, and I needed to check the account books, which was the part of his new enterprise Dermot found most difficult. I needn't have worried. Deidra had appointed herself office manager and was tackling the work with the same enthusiasm she gave to pounding dough.

She was on the phone to one of my major customers as I walked through the door and I winced as she yelled:

"For fucks sake, get thy arse into gear. That bloody delivery'll be in thy loading bay at nine sharp. I'll leave the rest to thee. Think you can manage that?" and she slammed the receiver into its cradle. How could you not laugh? I could hear Claire chortling behind me.

"'ello strangers," Deidra grinned up at us. "Just puttin' some jumped-up school kid in 'is place. [1]He'll shape up once he's lost the plum in 'is gob."

"Deidra, you're a tonic. Give me a hug," Claire said to the woman who had once laid her on her bottom with a left hook.

We sat on the office steps in the sunshine.

"What do I call thee now, Missus?" said Deidra, "I've been chewing it over for weeks and blow me if I can come to a decision. Ar't Margaret - like Mrs. Graham says - Meg or…. "

"She's Mrs. Greenwood," Claire cut in.

"Aye. She might be Mrs. Greenwood, but she'll allus be Meg to *me* - I've decided."

Deidra considered for a moment before she continued:

[1]*He'll be okay once he learns to speak properly*

Witch Stones

[1]"But I'll go to't foot of our stairs afore any of them 'oo-ligans down there'll call thee anything but Mrs. Green-wood."

It didn't escape me what kudos the familiarity would give her with the laborers and town's folk. It wasn't lost on Claire either.

"Now, t'books."

Deidra got up purposefully and strode up the steps to what used to be Dermot's office. Judging by the jug of flowers on the window sill, she'd clearly got a permanent foot in the door.

With difficulty she hefted a couple of tomes labelled 'Ins' and 'Outs' off a shelf, and thumbed through them muttering until she found the right pages.

The books had been immaculately kept in double entry fountain pen, with a ticked total at the end of each page. I looked at Claire. If these were right, the profits had gone up by twenty per cent. Dermot had clearly earned his right to a stake in the business.

"Better than thy sloppy work, ain't they?" she said. My God, but they were! By a mile.

"There's folders in 'ere on t'customers...."

She pulled open a filing cabinet drawer on oiled runners.

[2]... and in 'ere ar't suppliers although some of them'll be

[1]But I'll be damned if any of those hooligans down there'll call you anything but Mrs. Greenwood.
[2]and in here are the suppliers, although some of them'll be getting fired by the month's end if they don't improve.

goin' west by't month's end if they don't buck up."

I didn't doubt it for a moment.

"Well, I can see you've got everything well in hand," said Claire in the understatement of the year. "How does a twenty percent pay rise in line with profits sound?"

I was about to double it when Claire stepped hard on my foot.

"Grand - I'll look forward to it," smiled Deidra.

With the agreement of his three fellow shareholders, Guy had formally offered Dermot the stakeholder status he'd been tentatively promised.

Chapter Forty-nine

Why Valerie Became Mrs. Mitford-Clarke

Over the next few weeks I managed to get the rest of the story of the Elliots out of Claire, although it had been God's own job.

Once fifteen year old Valerie had disappeared to school in Carlisle to finish her education, Matt almost killed my astounded dad with the beating he gave him. He threatened him with swift judgement should he show his face in Nethershaw again or make any attempt to contact Valerie.

While Valerie was at school, she met the son of her geography teacher, a refined lad several years older than her called Hugo Mitford-Clarke. He fell passionately in love with the beautiful young girl, and she became fond of him. Fond mind, no more.

Her time away had been very hard on Valerie. She not only missed her family and the majesty of the fells and valleys she'd grown up in, but desperately longed for my baby brother. She felt uprooted and adrift.

On completion of her studies, Hugo was devastated when she told him she intended returning to Nethershaw. When he discovered Luneside House with its green slate and beautiful formal gardens had come on the market, he decided to press his suit and asked Valerie to marry him.

What could have been better? A wealthy husband offering her a mansion to live in, and a way out of her dilemma with her cousin.

The Elliots themselves closed ranks, and what they perceived as their shame was never alluded to. How could it be? My dad had been well and truly warned off, we were too young to know anything, Claire herself was imprisoned at Bythwaite, and Richard would rather have died than let his wife's infidelity become the subject of common gossip.

Valerie and Hugo had walked down the aisle in the luxury of Carlisle Cathedral, with all the pomp and panoply that involved. When she returned to Nethershaw she was no longer an Elliot.

The one fly in the ointment was Luneside's nearness to Nethershaw; but Valerie was unknown to the youngsters of the town, and if the older folk noticed her resemblance to Matthew they said nothing. She had been a nervous young girl of fifteen when she'd left Nethershaw, but an accomplished and confident young woman on her return.

To make doubly certain of her discretion, Valerie's mother insisted she employ Matthew as gardener at Luneside. And there he remained, watchful.

When Jennifer was born within the year, and christened at the local church, the inhabitants welcomed a family they considered gentry to their town, and from then on Valerie's life became a social imprisonment different, but as extreme as Claire's.

Then my father was killed, and very quickly my siblings disappeared; Ellen to Kendal shoe-works and marriage and John to the military. I was left alone at Fairview.

I don't know if it was for love of my brother or kindness for my situation, but when Miss Richardson, the schoolmaster's sister, discussed my predicament with her, Valerie told her she'd recently lost her housemaid and was willing to offer me the job.

I already knew the rest of course, but for one very important detail which the whole world seemed to have missed - including 'Bobby' Ryder to whom it was related.

It was pitch black in the garden shed when Matt had entered and found a young girl rehanging tools on their hooks. Believing it to be me as I helped often in the garden, in a moment of madness aimed at someone whose father he thought had ruined his cousin's life and destroyed their family's standing in the town, he decided to get even by ripping off my knickers and violently ravishing me under cover of night.

Unfortunately for Jenny he'd got the wrong girl, and it was at that point her father, closely followed by the minister made his discovery. He, of course, knew immediately it was Jennifer and acted accordingly.

"The rest you know," said Claire, white as a sheet and shaking.

"Now you know exactly why there was a body in your water barrel and who put it there and for what reason."

Chapter Fifty

Claire and Deidra Take on Valerie

I was now very rarely required at work and Claire not at all, although she did enjoy looking over the books with Deidra from time to time.

Deidra had employed the doctor's receptionist and Mrs. Wilson's granddaughter from the chapel to do the day to day running of the office. I hoped they, as Claire and I had done, would see past the brash exterior to the golden heart within.

It was yet another of those peaceful moments in my life, the ones as elusive as a kingfisher's dart.

Claire and I had been visiting Ghyll Howe and decided to pick up some groceries from the farmers' market in Nethershaw on our way home. We gave Deidra a lift into town as she'd shopping to do herself.

Claire was humming happily as she poked her way through a box of tomatoes picking out the best ones, when there was a tap on her shoulder, and she turned to find herself nose to nose with Valerie Mitford-Clarke.

This wasn't the delicate Claire of their last meeting on that very spot, nor the woman she had surprised on a picnic at Ghyll Howe. Claire was now a confident, successful business woman with more clout than the Mitford-Clarkes, and that extended throughout Westmoreland and beyond. Claire shook off Valerie's hand and glared at her.

"How can I help you, Mrs. Mitford-Clarke," said Claire in a voice which carried across the entire market square.

"Did you tell her? Did you tell Meg what you'd done? Does she know now what a tart you really are?" screeched Valerie, totally disregarding my presence.

Claire pulled me forward, her tone becoming icy.

"Not that conversations between my niece and me are any of your concern, but yes, I did. I gave her the whole un-expurgated version so you are quite welcome to ask her anything you like."

The marketplace was silent, the shoppers frozen to attention.

Deidra sauntered over smiling benignly, always a danger signal. She'd heard Valerie's loud voice and came to see what was going on.

"Morning, Mrs. Mitford-Clarke," she smiled genially, "So who's a tart?"

This was an increasingly dangerous situation.

"This jumped-up madame," sneered Valerie.

"Who? Mrs. Graham?"

This time the smile put me in mind of a hand-grenade with the pin pulled.

Deidra's arm shot out and held Valerie's neck in a vice-like grip.

"You surely do have a death wish you stupid fool," she said in a controlled tone I'd never heard before. She'd just completed a whole furious sentence without the use of a single swear-word.

"Now sod off afore I call PC Ryder."

Valerie straightened her tweed skirt, and walked head held high across the square to the sound of hilarious laughter from Deidra.

Peter Mitford-Clarke chose not to involve himself in women's affairs, swiveled round in the drivers' seat of his Jag parked inconspicuously behind a market stall and pushed open the door. Valerie climbed in and Peter whisked her out of harm's way - well, out of Deidra's way at least. Blood hadn't been spilled on this occasion, but I knew for a fact this was not the end of the matter.

After their release from prison, if the whereabouts of Hugo Peter Mitford-Clark had been downplayed, the Reverend Tim Robertshaw had disappeared into thin air.

It may just have been that the Council of Bishops drew the line at stuffing deceased gardeners into water receptacles, or he may just have decided missionary work in Africa was more his style. It was safe to say, on his release no-one in the Nethershaw area ever clapped eyes on him again.

As for the Mitford-Clarkes, over a period of weeks from Valerie's confrontation with Claire and Deidra, they discreetly packed away their belongings, and Madge Elliot told Deidra they'd returned to Carlisle. Only after they'd gone did an estate agent's sign appear nailed to the gate.

They'd been good to me when I'd needed help most, and unintentionally I'd been the cause of so much anguish for them. My friend Jennifer was no longer my friend because of it, and for that I was sorriest of all.

Chapter Fifty-one
Deidra's Proposal

Life returned to normal for us.

At Scarsdale the hay was safely gathered in. It had been something of a struggle as the late summer was wet, so we only managed one crop that year.

The apple trees in the orchard behind the house were now so old, some of them had had to be cut down for winter kindling. In the spring I'd plant new ones. Even so, a good crop of Bramleys was collected and stored on hemp sheets under the house eves.

Last year's lambs were brought to graze close to the farm to escape the worst of the weather.

In view of what had happened to his father, Guy wanted to send me to Bythwaite when the weather began to close in, but I wouldn't hear of it. I quoted 'for better or worse' to him, then thought and added 'for richer or poorer'.

"In sickness and in health," he added.

"Exactly."

By this time I was leaving Ghyll Howe almost entirely in Dermott's hands. Nevertheless, I paid a quick visit while I still could. The twins had now been well and truly sucked into the agricultural business.

Robbie was a teenager and had been courting under the rightly suspicious eye of his mother, as I was to learn.

I sat with my feet up on the kitchen table, swinging my chair back until Deidra who had brought the books for me to check, 'accidentally' kicked one of the legs away and I ended on my arse on the slate floor.

"Oops! Sorry. Good year," she said, sitting down. "Wet back end but it

didn't trouble us much. Not as good as last quarter - obviously - but up on t'same quarter last year."

"I don't need to look at those. Put them away and put the kettle on."

"Good idea! I've something to ask thee anyway so it's as good now as later."

Robbie wandered in and picked up an apple from a bowl on the dresser.

"'ower y'doin', Meg?" he asked cheekily.

I honestly believed he might have learned better. His mother stood up, threw his apple in the fireplace and clipped him round the ear - repeatedly. By this time she'd to stand on her toes to do it, since Robbie was over six foot and Deidra was five foot six in her stocking feet. It didn't stop him running like a scared rabbit.

"Good riddance!" she yelled at his fast-retreating back.

"Did yer know he'd got t'lass from t'chemist in[1] t'family way? One of these days [2]I'll swing f'that lad!

"Her dad wanted to hush it up and send her to some witch in a back street o' Kendal, but more lasses go in there as come out, and I wouldn't wish that on her through the stupidity of that bone-head," she said, motioning at the

[1]*pregnant*
[2]*hang for murdering him*

door with her thumb. "So she went to see [1]the quack and he put her right. It'll be a while afore he's walking another girl, I can tell thee."

Poor Robbie.

"So what's your question?" I asked her.

"Dermot and I were thinkin'.... now yer settled at Scarsdale, if maybe we might move in here."

She stopped and waited. When I didn't speak she continued:

"It's bigger and warmer than t'other place. I'd still keep a room f'thee - don't fret."

"And what do you propose doing with *your* house?" I asked.

"I thought we'd turn it into a bunkhouse for t'lads. There's a fair few now so they're coming from further away."

"Dear Lord, Deidra. That house cost a small fortune and you want to turn it into a youth hostel?"

"Why not?" she said.

The O'Connor family opened up the part of the house I'd never used and shifted their belongings in. It was to become a permanent home for them and I was glad of it. I couldn't have wished for better and more committed workers or just plain good friends. To put them in charge

[1]*the doctor*

of the farm I'd sweated blood for, for all those years was a privilege.

On my next visit several weeks later when I saw what they'd made of the old place, I was gob-smacked. They'd stripped it out down to bare stone, and Dermot and his boys had replastered and redecorated it.

There were new soft furnishings and beds in the six bed-rooms. That treadle must have been smoking.

The office was moved indoors from the yard and a small waiting-room constructed [1]'fer't nobs':

"Let the buggers wait."

Deidra's pride and joy was what she called her 'front room' which according to Robbie was being kept for the Queen's next visit to Nethershaw.

[2]"Cut it out wit watter-works. Tha'll set me off, yer daft cow," said Deidra, sniffing into her hankie as I teared up.

[1]*for the upper-class visitors*
[2]*Stop crying*

Chapter Fifty-two

The Bythwaite Fright

That Christmas, Guy and I spent at our own hearth-side. As winters went, it wasn't too bad, certainly it didn't compare to the year his father died.

We had a few days incarceration, which we spent roasting chestnuts and cuddling up before a roaring fire.

Spring, when it arrived, was a magical one with a cool wind but wall to wall sunshine which lit up the hills and rimed the primroses and daffodils with purest gold.

The river, still swollen, trilled and gurgled over its pebble bed and eddied round the mossy pilings of the pack bridge.

Claire and Joe visited us a time or two and we ate Sunday roast with them more often as the weather picked up.

The two men were involved with their respective farms, so I drove my accounts books over to Bythwaite, and Claire and I spent combined time on paperwork.

On one of the few occasions Guy and I stayed overnight at Bythwaite, Joe was awoken by one of the ground-floor sashes being surreptitiously raised and soft footsteps in the hall.

His shotgun was housed in a cabinet in the office at the back of the house, so he made his way there, closing the door noiselessly behind him while he loaded the gun.

As he edged along the hall towards the window directly below his room, he heard a pronounced gasp and was almost startled into dropping the gun,

Less guarded footsteps made a dash for the front door and a shadowy figure bolted outside before Joe recovered enough to react. Once he'd run out into the yard, a sudden gust blew the door shut with a loud bang which shocked the rest of us awake.

An even louder crack rent the air as Joe took a shot at the interloper.

By the time he walked back indoors, the rest of us were collected in a huddle at the foot of the stairs.

"I lost sight when he ran out of the yard security lighting," said Joe. "I thought I saw a shadow on the stile but I could be wrong. In any case, we'd never find anyone in the fields in the dark.

As Joe was talking, out of the corner of my eye I glimpsed Claire pick something up from the floor, glance at it and push it hastily into her pocket.

"Did you recognize him? Could you tell how tall he was or his build?" asked Guy.

"Not really - before I'd grasped the situation he was gone. I say he, but from the way he ran it might just as well have been a woman. They were gone in a flash. I heard a distinct gasp before they bolted, which a man doesn't usually do."

"What were they after do you think?" I asked.

"No idea. There's no cash in the house other than that in the safe in the office. The books are in there too."

Bythwaite is a bit secluded for it to be a random theft," I mused. "It's five miles to the nearest house. They must have been looking for something in particular."

"Whatever the case," said Joe. "There's nothing we can do now. We'll have to wait for daylight. Let's go back to bed."

We did but I doubt anyone closed their eyes, except Guy who snored softly for the rest of the night.

Chapter Fifty-three

The Missing Photo

The following morning, Guy had to go home to see to the animals so he was off by six o'clock and Joe wasn't much after.

'Cilla' deposited breakfast on the table for Claire and me and disappeared back to the kitchen whistling an ear-piercing 'Anyone Who Had a Heart."

"I'm going to have to fire that girl," said Claire with a grimace as she spread marmalade on her toast.

"Don't you dare. She does more to brighten my day than anyone. I have a great time trying to imagine who she'll be next."

Once our work was done, Claire and I decided to take a look along the lane and on the fields over the stile to see if we could find anything of the night's intruder. There was nothing except a lace-trimmed handkerchief which had blown into one of the hay racks, and silver paper from a chocolate wrapper which was hardly conclusive either. There was nothing else at all, not even a footprint.

Spring is a hectic time on a farm with all hands on deck, fifteen hour days and nights often interrupted during lambing, so it was a good while until the Grahams and Greenwoods met up again. The incident of the intruder was quickly forgotten, until a friend of Joe's whose animals grazed adjoining pastures, mentioned that one of his workers had come across an old car which appeared to have been abandoned close to his yard. The Springtime profusion had covered it in weeds until it was barely distinguishable from the hedgerow.

He went to take a look, but it'd been robbed of anything useful for identification. The number-plates had been rived off and there were no personal belongings other than a much-thumbed road map of Westmoreland. He'd better things to think of at the time he said impatiently, when he came to recount the tale later.

Although she had servants, Claire had a penchant for feather dusters. She must have had a dozen of them in an assortment of colors. Bizarrely she could identify every bird they'd come from and would recite turtle dove, jay, ostrich - that was the biggest - pigeon and assorted others.

She was flitting around the sitting room one morning, humming to herself and giving the occasional pirouette when she made a discovery she was hard-pressed to explain.

When she came to dust the mantlepiece, she moved her beloved silver framed photo of my dad and discovered the picture in it had changed. In place of her favorite shot of 'the handsome hero', was the faded one of him on a French beach.

What upset her most wasn't the loss of the picture, but the fact she couldn't remember the last time she'd seen it. I comforted her with the thought she had spent weeks sorting and reframing the pictures in the box. Perhaps she'd accidentally switched them round.

Was her absentmindedness returning? She sat down and cried. She feared that more than anything else.

"There's no need for that Claire. You've been so taken up with sorting the other photos," I laughed shakily, "You probably changed that one without thinking."

"No," she said emphatically, then more uncertainly. "Anyone else but not Robert. I could never forget Robert no matter how distracted I was."

But the fact remained that the picture was not only not in the frame, but missing altogether and she couldn't be certain about her actions. I sat with her, but she gazed out of the window and didn't notice when I left to speak to Joe on his return.

Much against my inclination, I'd to go back to Scarsdale. I spoke to Guy on the phone and he needed my help on a matter of some urgency or I'd have stayed.

It was agreed Joe would work things out so he'd stay home for a couple of days, then I could take over again.

Whenever we were apart, Guy was always especially attentive afterwards, which usually rapidly became amorous.

Once the workers had gone home in the evenings, we christened the hay field which was prickly from its first mowing, then various rooms in the house, including the pantry.

One evening when he'd been particularly rampant, and I'd been as giggly, we visited the Sisters. We'd been there before but I was always nervous of the place.

He'd grabbed my hand and we were half-way up the lane to the ridge before I knew it.

Guy ran so fast I was beginning to lose my footing. When he realized he stopped, kissed me ardently and then continued to run, pausing now and then to help me across the edge of the scree slope.

I was so relieved when we saw the ghostly Sisters glimmering in the moonlight.

Chapter Fifty-four

Valerie's Despicable Declaration

I'd never been anywhere before or since quite like the Seven Sisters. To say they were mysterious or even creepy just doesn't cover it.

I think the closest I can get is to say they were ancient. Not old as a person would be, but immortal as the peaks of [1]the Pennines, strange, immutable, eternal.

They carry so much ambiance that as you stare at them in wonder, they stare right back. It's very unnerving.

This is why I wasn't keen on love-making there. It was as if the stones surrounding us were watching, judging.

Guy wasn't as fanciful as I. He was a farmer, a man of the earth, probably closer to the nature of the stones than most people.

So it was that we, he with gusto and I with initial unease, played kiss-chase around the Sisters until we flopped to the ground, panting with laughter.

There was a clearly audible 'crunch' and Guy looked down to see the remains of a skeletal hand which had dropped over his shoulder, bones stretched and covered here and there in brittle parchment.

The scream I let loose could have been heard by the lawyer in Kendall. Guy jumped to his feet brushing down his clothes as if he was covered in poisonous spiders.

The bones behind him clattered to the earth like so many

[1] *a mountain range sometimes referred to as the backbone of England.*

dominoes, held together in places by the remains of shrunken ligaments and clothing.

We went down one hell of a lot faster than we went up, every so often sliding on loose stones, regaining our footing and running only to slip and fall again.

Guy was, and still is, a generous and kind human being, and once we

got home and could breathe again, he sat me down, took my hand across the table and said:

"We have to go back. That was once a human being. We can't leave them out in the cold… to rot."

I must have looked as sick as I felt.

"Come on. We can do this, but seriously if you're not up to it, I can soon drop you with Claire, and Joe and I will see to covering the body up."

That sounded a much better idea.

At Bythwaite we explained our grisly discovery to Joe and Claire.

"I'm sorry, I just can't face it again," I apologized, shame-faced. Guy kissed me and whispered in my ear:

"It's sometimes comforting to feel you need protecting. Makes me feel strong and virile."

He chuckled but was suddenly serious.

"Whoever it turns out to be, must have been there for weeks to be in that state. There's virtually nothing left of…"

It was at that point I bolted for the lavatory, and when I returned Joe and Guy had gone.

Claire stared into the fire for a few seconds.

"I think I know who it is."

She handed me an envelope with Joe's name on it.

"I picked it up from the floor in the hall when whoever-it-was fled through the door the evening of the break-in. Read it."

I drew out the three sheets of paper inside. The grandfather clock in the dark hall whirred and struck the hour.

"You don't know me Joseph, but I am cousin to Matthew Elliot who was accidentally killed by my husband and his friend and concealed at Meg Graham's allotment.

As no-one else - for shame - will admit the facts to you, I feel I must acquaint you with the circumstances of your birth.

You are not, as you suppose, the son of Richard and Claire Armstrong Graham. Your father was Robert Graham, Richard's brother. You were born of an affair between your mother and her brother-in-law."

My hand flew to my mouth and I gasped:

Witch Stones

"I know this because I caught them at Fairview after Robert's wife, who was also Claire's sister, had died. It was shortly after the birth of Robert and Moira's son, John.

Robert, living on the fells in poverty, was left to care for three children when Claire's sister died: Ellen, the eldest who now resides abroad, Margaret - Meg - with whom you are well acquainted and my darling Johnny, who left to join the army at the age of fifteen and hasn't been heard from since.

As a Christian act I undertook to care for the new baby - John - until Robert was back on his feet after his wife's death. I offered to take Maggie too but he was ashamed to hand Johnny over to me as it was.

The only other person in Nethershaw who knew the truth of John's identity was my mother. When the gossip became insupportable for her, Johnny was returned to his father for good, and I was sent away to school in Carlisle.

Before I left and as I was returning John to Fairview for the final time, I was horrified to find Robert in his marital bed with your mother. I caught them in the act, of that there was absolutely no doubt. I assumed Claire had returned to Beckton where you were born..

Of course, you could have been Richard's child, except Robert told me otherwise. He had no shame that he'd defiled his marriage. He said Claire was the love of his life and that he couldn't deny her.

Robert admitted to me the affair, without Moira's knowledge, had been going on since Richard and Claire's wedding. Once Moira had died they were free to do as they wished.

Well, there you have it. I pity anyone whose mother is a whore, his father a liar and who is himself a bastard, holding all his possessions by fraud. I thought it was wrong, knowing what I did, that you continue in ignorance of your situation.

Yours very truly…"

And it was signed *'Valerie Elliot Mitford-Clarke'.*

For a moment I was open-mouthed. Then Claire said seriously:

"Do you hate me, Meg? I could bare all the rest but that."

"Of course I don't - you'd already told me the gist. This disgraceful letter only adds detail.

Chapter Fifty-five

Joe's Eyes are Opened.

Our conversation was cut short when my brother and his brother-in-law - Lord, that sounded strange - entered the hall, discarding coats and blowing on chapped hands.

"It was too dark to see much, but from the remains of the clothing and small bones, I'd have guessed it was a woman," said Guy poking the sitting room fire and sending sparks flying up the chimney. "I don't know of anyone who's gone missing recently, do you Joe?"

I gave Claire a meaningful look.

"It might as well be now. Prevarication won't make it go away," I said, talking over the top of Joe's reply.

"Sounds ominous," said Joe at our nervous expressions, his own trepidation hidden behind a cheery smile.

"What's up, Meg?" asked Guy when Claire and I remained mute.

"I'll be in my room," said Claire, stuffing the letter in my hand and making a dash for the door.

"Well, I'll be... "

"You sure will," I said, handing Valerie's letter to Joe, and disappearing upstairs myself. Courage was no more my strong point than Claire's.

The two of us sat upstairs, gripping each other's hands and waiting for the fall-out which ten minutes later still hadn't happened. There was just the quiet click of the front door opening and closing.

Witch Stones

"I can't stand this a minute longer," said my aunt. "It's too quiet - he should be roaring round the house and calling me all the names under the sun by now."

Guy was standing expressionless in the middle of the sitting room when we went downstairs.

"You'd better go find him, Meg. He said he was going for a walk but its nearly midnight and he had no coat. I'll stay with Mrs. Graham."

"Be nice to her," I warned Guy, but there was no need. Within ten minutes, I'd no doubt at all she'd be sobbing on his shoulder.

I found Joe almost immediately, striding up and down the lane, his expression indistinct in the security lighting's glare. He seemed to be holding his breath and panting at the same time so it didn't take long for him to collapse on the field-side stile, head in hands.

I knew this was something all of us must face now or it would fester. I went indoors again and snatched the letter from Guy's hand. By this time, Claire was downstairs in her robe sobbing into his shoulder as I'd foreseen.

Armed with the letter I gritted my teeth and went out once more to see Joe.

"Right, let's start from the beginning and go through this letter point by point.

"You don't *know* Valerie. You don't *know* her husband or Matt Elliot either. I can tell you about them but so far there's nothing there to concern you.

"Next - she surely had taken a lot upon herself. The relationship between you and your parents has fuck-all to do with her."

He bowed his head in acknowledgement.

"The next paragraph's true. You're not Uncle Dick's son - a fact I'd have thought would delight you. You're the son of his brother Robert, who by all accounts was a good human being - even his mother thought so."

"And I'm supposed to be okay with that?" he frowned.

"You bet your life you are, you berk. If I can swallow it, so can you."

That seemed to take the wind out of his sails. Particularly as he'd worked himself into such a state his brain had largely stopped functioning.

"For God's sake, Joe. Your mother's Claire Armstrong Graham and mine is Moira Armstrong Graham. Both of us have Robert Graham for a father, which makes us…"

I moved my arm in a winding motion to get the cogs whirring in his brain.

"Well, dumb-cluck?"

He sat up straight and the panic faded from his eyes as intelligence returned.

"Good God! You're my *sister*?"

He sat still for a moment and I saw his fingers twitch slightly as he thought his way through it.

"No. Half-sister."

"Can we carry on?"

"No need. Don't care how it happened, that's just the best. Sister! Wow! I have a sister. I've always been a lonely only child. That's great!"

He picked me up and threw me in the air. I slapped his face.

"Get off! We're going through the rest of it whether you like it or not.

"After her sister died, shortly after the birth of my brother John, your mother and our father continued the several years of bonking round Westmoreland which had begun at Claire and Richard's wedding.

"Valerie took it upon herself - something she was good at in the name of Christianity - to care for baby John... I can't be bothered with the rest - you read the letter. Deal with it."

I left him, letter in hand to chew the matter over and returned to the house.

Chapter Fifty-six

Meg and Dead Body Number Three

"He won't be long. It's bloody freezing out there," I said and as I spoke Joe strode in and knelt at his mother's knee, kissing her hands.

As we Greenwoods left them time and space, Guy said:

"We'll leave the body at the Sisters until the morning, shall we? She won't be going anywhere. Goodnight."

The following morning the table hadn't been set for breakfast.

"Sarah - we can't eat breakfast on a bare table," yelled Joe. "Move your arse. Chop, chop!"

[1]"Keep yer 'air on, Mr. Joe."

Better than usual - marginally - but I could see my brother was impressed she'd remembered his name.

Over tea and toast, we discussed what to do about the body at the Sisters.

"Why don't you ring Deidra and check if Valerie has been sighted in the Nethershaw district?" Joe suggested.

"I thought she and Peter had gone to Carlisle. So why would she be here? Doesn't seem likely."

When I spoke to Deidra on the phone, my question prised her because she *had* thought she'd seen Valerie.

[1]*Don't flap*

shopping in the town. It was only a glimpse she said, so she couldn't be certain. Of course she may have been visiting her aunts, but Deidra wouldn't know.

The body, now little more than a pile of loosely connected bones, was spread on the turf beneath the smallest stone like a Geppetto puppet.

When Guy had sat on it, the body had plummeted sideways and in the tattered coat pocket was a piece of card, perhaps six or seven inches long. I made to pick it up but remembered Joe's warning about disturbing a crime scene when Josh Greenwood had died.

When the time came, my husband and I took the police to the Sisters. The stones now made me more nervous than ever. It must have been a trick of the light, but they seemed to be leaning slightly inwards. The blank eyes of the skull stared back.

I wondered what Guy would tell the detective as to why we'd gone to a stone circle in the middle of the night. He craftily side-stepped - almost.

"Mr. Graham and I had business in Beckton and when we returned we walked the fields to check his stock. My wife came with us.

"By this time it had become dark, so Mr. Graham went back home, and Margaret and I sat down next to the Stones to rest before making our way back to Bythwaite." He reddened and coughed. "You'll appreciate we're not long married.

Witch Stones

"As I leaned my back against the stone there was a terrible crunching noise and the body's arm and hand shot over my shoulder and scared the both of us half to death.

"When I knocked the body, it slid sideways and there was something falling out of the pocket. See?"

He moved to shift one of the heavier bones with his foot.

"No - no sir. Don't disturb it, this may be a crime scene. It's secure for now. We'll remove it later."

Thank goodness this had happened at the Seven Sisters and not in Nethershaw.

The inquest would still be in Kendal, but in another building and with the county Coroner rather than a judge. I breathed a sigh of relief - the last one thought I was Lizzie Borden.

As no-one knew who the body belonged to, and we had been the ones to discover it, Guy and I were present at the hearing in place of a relative.

The police testimony held information new to me. The bones of the wrists had faint V-shaped grooves in them, so it looked as if they had been cut with a knife which made the death in all likelihood a suicide.

A knife was presented in evidence, a razor-sharp curved farm item which was used for trimming skin from meat. It must have been found nearby and we'd missed it.

What had happened to the card from the pocket of the jacket? It may have been a clue to the woman's identity, and no mention of it was made. If the police hadn't found it, it must have been removed by one of us. No-one else had been there.

The victim went unidentified, other than it was a woman in her fifties with short dark hair. The case remained open.

If Claire was right, and I was sure she was, this had to be Valerie Mitford-Clarke.

Chapter Fifty-seven
Meg's Introduction to Molly

A couple of days later we were due to leave for Scarsdale, and while Guy was loading our belongings into the back of the Land Rover and he and Joe were chatting, Claire cut flowers from her greenhouse to take to church. It was a bit out of character, I'd never judged her to be a religious person.

"Get in," she said to me and without further ado we set off down the lane to Beckton.

The church where I was married was set amongst green fields on the Bythwaite side of Beckton. It was surrounded by an unkempt burial yard of lichen-coated stones leaning at various angles.

That Claire had been here more often than I thought was apparent from the way she breezed into the vestry and picked up three ugly metal pots. Filling them with water she began to dump the flowers in with no care whatever for their arrangement.

Tied in another bunch with a raffia bow was a carefully arranged bouquet of roses.

"Come on, as a Graham there is something you should know."

"If it entails another emotional shock Claire, I'd rather you kept it to yourself. I don't think I could deal with anything else."

She grabbed my hand and marched straight to the back of the church to a pair of graves set several feet apart. When

I say straight… I mean straight. Straight over the grave of Uncle Dick and several others.

The left hand grave belonged to Joseph Graham of Bythwaite who had died June 2nd 1926. Presumably that was Uncle Dick and my dad's father.

My grandmother, Molly, whose birthname I saw was Mary, had a rather different memorial from her husband. The headstone read:

To the memory of our beloved Molly Graham
Late of Bythwaite Farm, Beckton.
Born Mary Elizabeth Carrick in Dumfries
Scotland April 1st 1890
Died Bythwaite May 31st 1937

"If anyone was to dig this grave, they would find it empty," said Claire. "Molly is buried with those she believed to be her sisters on the hill above Bythwaite.

"The circle is so remote and so little visited that no-one ever noticed that in 1937 instead of the Seven Sisters there were eight. Josh Greenwood and I took the coffin there. Robert didn't yet know Molly had died.

"Of course, all this happened in the dead of night when I could climb over the trellis on my garden wall unseen."

Claire gently propped the bouquet against the stone and stood away.

"She thought herself to be one of the Dumfries Coven of Witches, descendants of those persecuted by Mary of Scots in the sixteenth century. I'm not saying it's correct

- just that she fervently believed it herself. Even if Molly's claims seem far-fetched, it's absolutely true you are in tune with nature. Birds and butterflies come to you as if you were a magnet; trees look greener, flowers brighter. These things I know to be true - I've seen them myself.

"Perhaps Molly was right after a fashion. Not only this, but you are an exceptionally lucky person, otherwise how could you possibly have gone from your beginnings to where you are now?"

That I absolutely couldn't argue with - I'd often thought it myself.

"I go through this little ritual from time to time," said Claire, "Molly was kind to me when no-one else was. I have no other way of commemorating her - I can't put flowers up at the circle.

"She was light of heart and had a mischievous sense of humor. She was sick to death of her dull husband but as was the only course of action for a woman in those days, she gritted her teeth and stuck by him. He probably took the cake as the most tedious person I ever met in my life. When he died she dumped him in the grave yard and never went back."

"Molly knew Richard was a complete bastard, but she misjudged what a malicious monster he could be. As soon as his father died, Richard in a fit of jealousy threw Robert out of Bythwaite, and when he realized he'd been cuck-olded for years and now I was carrying Robert's child, he shoved me in that plush prison you rescued me from.

"Molly loathed Richard for the rest of her life for taking Robert from her, and when she learned the truth of my child, she became my devoted friend. Joe replaced his father in her affections.

"Perhaps now you understand why I felt only relief when I shot Richard. He destroyed Robert's life, mine and his mother's with no regret at all. I hope he rots in hell as he deserves."

Claire snatched the bouquet back from the empty grave and grabbed my hand.

"I'm sick to death of all this secrecy. Come on."

She drove back to Bythwaite and practically ran me up the hill to the Sisters, bypassing my husband and Joe.

"Here you are Molly," she said in front of the smallest stone, and placed the lovely flowers at its base. "To hell with the rest of them. These are from me and Meg, for you,"

Just as suddenly as it had flared, her temper died and with delicate fingers Claire carefully removed a rose bud from Molly's grave and put it in my hand.

"If you accept your grandmother's beliefs, you must know her gifts only run down the female line. She had no daughters of her own. She never knew you and Ellen, so died believing she was the last of her line."

Claire held my hand hard against Molly's stone and the vibration it gave off nearly knocked me off my feet.

She hooted with laughter.

"Sometimes things happen which make me wonder if what she believed wasn't quite as far-fetched as I

imagine. Witches were notoriously - or should I say glo-
riously - good at sex. By the strength of Molly's reaction
I think we can safely assume you're carrying another little
Greenwood - and a girl at that!

"Let's go - Guy'll be wondering where you are."

Chapter Fifty-eight

Would it be Kinder to Let Things Be?

Once home and having had time to consider, I was mortified by Claire's story. My Lord! My life had completely veered off-track.

How was I going to tell my husband I may not be only Meg Graham Greenwood as he believed, but a quarter Morgana Le Fey on my Graham side? He'd die laughing so I kept the thought to myself. There was no saying any of it was fact anyway. Claire seemed to hold no opinion one way or the other.

Several days later when Claire rang, I'd already devised a course of action:

"I need to go to Carlisle to check if Valerie's there with Peter just to rule her out. They were good to me once, I owe it to them to be sure of the facts."

"Is that wise, do you suppose? Even if she disappeared, do you think he'd be interested? If she was losing it she sure as hell wouldn't enhance his business standing in Carlisle."

"Guy may have a problem with all this too," I frowned.

"I think you'll probably find he won't. He and Joe are farmers and close to the earth. You shouldn't discount the fact that Guy chose to bury his own father in a cornfield rather than the churchyard."

"You think he'll do the 'witchy woman' thing, then?"

She rolled her eyes and tutted.

"No, of course he won't. Probably the only person who might understand is Deidra. She's Irish."

"By way of Westmoreland," I scoffed.

"Well, if you're really dying to tell someone, I'd guess Deidra is your best bet. After all 'hell'll freeze over before Dermot gets a word out of me' as she said when I swore her to secrecy over Joe."

"So what do I do about Valerie?"

Such was my unease I did drive to Ghyll Howe and after all that effort the only response I got was:

"I've got the kid's socks t' wash. Believe me if there were t' possibility of a chat I'd take it."

"Please - it's urgent."

"They'll not harm for a soaking, I suppose," she said grudgingly.

Paul was in my kitchen, which was now her own.

[1]"Here's a ten bob note. Cod 'n' chips twice and whatever yer dad wants. And I'll see t'change if yer don't mind."

In her mind all her children were still six.

We sat down and she waited. I wished she wouldn't do that - she never talked when she was supposed to and *vice versa*.

The recounting of events was as short as I could make it

[1]*Here's a ten shilling note. Fish and fries twice, and whatever your dad wants. Don't forget the change*

but nevertheless Paul was back with the chips before I'd finished. He was told to 'get lost'.

"Best tale I've 'eard in an age. 'ow much of it's true? And what were ye doing up there in t' middle of the night - no. don't tell me. I can figure that out."

"I'm not so bothered about the sorcery stuff - she can believe what she likes. What I want to know is what I do if it was Valerie on top of that hill and if I should speak to Peter. Claire seems to think it'll be alright to keep quiet but I don't think that's the point, do you?"

"Do you think t'old Elliot girls will know anything? When I thought I saw Mrs. M-C in t'shop I thought she might be staying with them. Worth a shot. Do you want to ask or shall I?"

"You go. You can scare the truth out of them."

"No, we're the best of friends. The new minister allows no nonsense from them. They won't hurt me."

Patience was definitely a virtue with Deidra.

There was an old bench under an enormous horse-chestnut tree opposite the stone cottage of the Misses Elliot. I sat there impatiently swinging my legs and waiting for Deidra to reappear. She seemed to be taking an age, but it was only twenty minutes before she reappeared, carrying an old wicker basket full of clinking bottles of 'nectar'.

"This has cost me a bloody fortune," she complained, looking with distaste at the contents of the bag.

"Stop grouching. You've never refused a glass or two before. What did they say?"

"I told them I thought I'd seen Valerie around the town. I was right and she'd outstayed 'er welcome. She was there for five days then said she was going home. That's where they thought she was.

"They said they'd ring Mr. Mitford-Clarke this evening. When it's cheaper."

At my look of incomprehension she added:

"Wealthy folk like thee don't know weekend and night calls cost less. It's a wonder *I* know now I'm counted among thee."

She straightened her shoulders and looked pleased with herself.

"Don't look so vexed," she continued. "Yer room's still there like I said, and I'd as well feed thee as the rest o' the gannets in t'digs."

The following morning Deidra returned some 'empties' to the elderly sisters, so she could continue her enquiries without sounding pushy.

Deidra pushy? Never.

This time she was longer - nearly forty minutes.

"Where the hell have you been? Dan Barber's driven past three times - two to see why his boss was sitting under a horse-chestnut on an old bench."

"Well this int about to [1]buck thee up. They've no idea. They rang but there was no reply. I thought he'd have had

[1]*cheer you up*

a maid or something but nobody answered."

The following day when I got back to Scarsdale, I discussed the meeting with the Elliot ladies with Guy - or at least I tried to.

"Valerie's aunts phoned Peter but he was out. I'd have had to wait another day for them to make a cheap evening call - did you know about that? Deidra said she'd tackle them again.

"I still think it wouldn't be right not to check on Valerie."

He left to tinker with his tractor.

"Even if it does turn out to be Valerie," said Claire, "Peter can only trace her to Nethershaw if he knew she'd gone to stay with her aunts. They could have told him Deidra was asking after her but that wouldn't mean anything."

All that was true. But it didn't make it right.

The still-living Greenwoods and Grahams stood well out of the way as the cortege went into the church, came out again sharpish, and the modest coffin was lowered into a hole in a churchyard which already held Richard and Joseph Graham. To add to the dismal scene it was raining the kind of depressing drizzle that often clouded the slopes of Aidafell.

Chapter Fifty-nine

Hugo Peter Mitford-Clarke Esq

I was up by four the following morning, before Guy was astir, and driving to Carlisle. I'd left him a note on the table. He wasn't going to like it. Neither was I but it had to be done.

Half way up the [1]A6 it dawned on me I hadn't the faintest idea where I went when I got to Carlisle. If Peter's choice was anything like Luneside House, it was likely to be in the countryside. This would be a problem as Carlisle was surrounded by countryside for miles. It was the County Town of Cumberland for a reason - there wasn't an alternative.

Carlisle was a disappointment for a city with a cathedral and a castle. Small and compact, its size was dictated by the remains of a substantial wall which bore testament to centuries of border unrest. It was in desperate need of an overhaul. The weather hadn't lifted and the mist-covered mountains had given way to smog-covered brick streets.

It's still entered by an enormous Tudor gateway which leads to a roughly triangular market place. To one side are a series of meandering medieval lanes of shops, and opposite a large Victorian hotel. Above all, towers the castle keep which still houses the county jail.

I parked my car on the square and checked into the depressing, but grandly-named 'Crown and Mitre Hotel'.

[1]*Main road from Kendal to Carlisle*

With my fingers crossed I telephoned Guy from a booth in the foyer. He was fit to be tied.

"Get back here NOW! I won't tell you again. If you're not here by tonight, I'll come and get you. What kind of wife sneaks out in the middle of the night?"

"One who doesn't want to listen to that crap from a bloody husband."

I hung up, tight-lipped and fuming.

The phone book seemed the logical place to start looking and I struck lucky straight away.

H P Mitford-Clarke, Willow Grange Farm, Crosby. Carlisle Tel. 4358

Farm? Peter had escaped Nethershaw to a FARM?

Raking out six pennies from my purse I called the number but like the two old dears in Nethershaw I got no reply, so I tried again. Nothing, so I put the money back in my purse and went to look round the shops to kill some time.

After four telephone attempts, and as it was still only early afternoon, I decided to drive to Crosby which turned out to be a pleasant little brick and white-wash village with two pubs - the source of all local knowledge in every village in the country.

I entered the first hostelry, appropriately named the 'Brickmaker's Arms' and ordered a drink in the lounge. My first attempt to engage the landlady in conversation was thwarted by constant interruptions from the taproom at the other end of the bar.

Eventually I managed to corner her and after discussing the weather, rock and roll - Del Shannon was playing loudly in the other bar - and the price of beer in post war Britain, I got round to the important stuff.

"I'm actually trying to find a Mr. Mitford-Clarke, he owns Willow Grange Farm I understand."

"Owned, dear. He died. Stroke, so I've been told."

"That's a shame," I said, pulling a sad face, "I'd some papers for him to sign. Perhaps his wife may be able to help."

Canny.

"No idea - she didn't come here often."

The landlady thought for a moment:

"No, it's some time since I saw her in the village either. I used to pass the time of day but I haven't seen her for quite a while. I've no idea where she went after her husband passed on."

I drove over to Willow Grange to be absolutely sure it was empty. It smelled of stale milk and manure, had shutters and a pretty purple clematis in much need of pruning, trained over the front door.

For the life of me I couldn't imagine Hugo Peter Mitford-Clarke donning wellies to muck out a [1]shippen, and Valerie was more the begonia type.

I had done my level best to make sure of the facts. Valerie had disappeared.

I was back at Scarsdale the next day to a dressing down

[1]*cow shed*

from my husband. After he'd run out of steam and I'd looked suitably contrite, we patched things up in the usual way, then went to Bythwaite so I could tell Claire what I'd learned.

She looked smug. Hadn't she told me to leave well enough alone? But she conceded she could understand my point of view.

Joe and Guy had stayed quiet in the background, but now Joe said:

"What's all the fuss about? It isn't as if you stuck a knife in her yourselves. Mum says nothing but she seems to think there's some truth in this abracadabra stuff. Perhaps she's right considering the missing picture is now back in its frame. Where'd you conjure that up from, Mother?"

Claire's face was the picture of innocence and I believed her until I remembered the piece of card in the tattered coat pocket. She must have taken it without anyone seeing. It had been the right shape and size for a photograph. Only Valerie would have stolen such a thing from Claire - only Valerie would have had reason.

"She wants to believe Molly because she finds it difficult to let her go," I said quickly, hoping they wouldn't notice I'd skipped all mention of

the photograph, "Which reminds me. Molly says there's a little Greenwood on the way - she thinks it's a girl."

"Molly's a corpse. She can't tell anyone anything," said Joe.

But he was wrong. Twelve months later there was a little scrap of bawling dampness lying in her daddy's arms.

Witch Stones

Guy struggled to stem the tears which threatened to flood his cheeks, as the vicar dubbed her Angela Mary Greenwood. Ironic it should be the Barber brat who gave me the idea, but the first person to call her Anj in my hearing would get severe ear-ache.

"If there's a follow-up and it's a boy, you're not calling 'im John-Claude," huffed Deidra, the Godmother, [1]"or I'll tek 'im to t'orfnidge me-sel."

Claire went alone to introduce Molly to her great-granddaughter. It seemed right - after all, it had been Claire who took Molly's body to the Stones, and later presented me to a woman I never knew, but whose spirit had infused my entire life.

I hoped Molly would come to care for our little Angel.

Another addition to the line of Dumfries Witches. Perhaps.

[1]*or I'll take him to the orphanage myself*

Chapter Sixty

Joining

And so began another generation of Greenwoods, and a cementing of the link between Bythwaite and Scarsdale. Angela carried the blood of both families in her veins.

One day when she was five or six years old, Angela Guy and I visited Bythwaite and after dinner I walked alone across the fields to the Sisters with Claire, as we often did. The view of my home across the fertile earth to the distant mountains was spectacular from the slope above. We spent many hours there in quiet contemplation, lost in our own thoughts.

On one particular day as we rounded the corner to the Sisters, Claire grabbed my arm and dragged me back.

We watched covertly as my little daughter wove, dancing round the Stones with a young woman. As they turned in our direction my mouth opened in astonishment. They were so alike the one resembled a miniature version of the other.

The woman saw us first, blew a kiss to Claire and smiling her bewitching smile, sank gracefully to the ground and disappeared.

Angela skipped over to us smiling broadly.

"Mama, did you see the lady? I'm so pleased you did. No-one's ever seen her but me. Now you have - and Auntie Claire too."

She took Claire's hand and skipped off down the hillside, smiling Molly's smile.

Witch Stones

I believe our daughter's birth touched something deep in Claire's heart. The keepers of each other's secrets, they spent more and more time alone at the Seven Sisters as Angela grew.

Joe continued to think his mother deluded, but he'd become so used to caring for her over the years, in his forties he still hadn't married. Angela's beloved father continued to pretend nothing was happening. We didn't argue - he was happier in his ignorance.

I wondered if in his heart of hearts Joe wasn't lonely in that remote farmhouse, with only his mother for company. He never seemed to be. He said he'd inherited a sister and all her bloody crew, he didn't need any more aggravation, so we left it at that.

But he also said he had come to understand why Dick had been so desperate to hang on to Bythwaite he'd locked up his wife, and bullied Joe himself until he was terrified of him.

It was the land, Joe said. The land spoke to him, and Guy understood his feelings I knew. This made our eight chipped rocks on a Westmoreland hillside seem a bit pathetic, even if they did buzz sexily from time to time.

As she grew, our daughter looked more and more like the photograph of Claire's beloved mother-in-law hanging in the hall at Bythwaite, the same dimpled mouth and cheeky smile, the same tiny waist and dainty ankles. She was the center of Guy's existence - everything he did, he did for her.

"She'll be worth a bob or two when she gets older. Might even attract one of Deidra's 'nobs' from London," he said.

"I wish you luck with that one," I replied dryly.

We'd no idea where Angela got her brains - Joe was the closest to an intellectual we had and that was only because he liked listening to Gershwin and reading the Financial Times. In all other respects, despite his university education, he was as clueless as the rest of us. But Angela excelled at so much she'd a problem deciding what to do.

In the end she chose to train as an archivist which baffled us. Claire said it was someone who looked after old books in dusty libraries and she'd end up an old maid. Her dad argued she was much too beautiful to be left on the shelf and couldn't understand why Claire and I collapsed laughing.

Much to Deidra's disgust Angela chose to become 'a nob from darn sarf' and took up a post at the British Library in London. At every visit to Nethershaw or Scarsdale, she was given a dressing down for her accent, I'd to remind Deidra she'd been born in Ireland and now had a Westmorland accent you could cut with a knife.

"I know," she sniffed "But here's here, and there's there."

On a bright June day, with all the house windows opened to a fragrant breeze, Claire and I took tea on our little bit of lawn at Scarsdale where I'd first met Josh Greenwood.

"Why didn't you have more children?" she asked me.

"Just never happened - like with you and Robert, I suppose. Joe was long in coming."

"Must have been Molly's fault," she laughed. "She got her carry-on witch and that was that."

She paused to sip her tea.

"Has Angela ever shown any leanings… you know…"

"She's never mentioned moving to Dumfries, no."

"Don't be silly Meg. You know what I mean…"

Joe and Guy pulled into the yard with a trailer containing a single ewe.

"Coughing," shouted Guy. "Best separate it out 'til we know what's what."

Joe wiped his shitty hands down his pants and helped himself to a buttered scone which he downed in one.

"Good Lord," scowled a fastidious Claire, "If that beast's infected you'll be sharing a pen. Go and wash up."

They'd only just disappeared through the house door when there was the sound of a loud car horn. A pale blue Cortina pulled up, and out jumped our beautiful daughter, all slender legs and shining curls.

In retrospect, I was a little surprised that as I rushed to hug her, Claire had remained in her seat. I flung my arms around Angela and kissed her repeatedly on both cheeks.

"Why didn't you say you were coming? We could have planned something - got Auntie Deidra over - maybe Dermot if he could be spared. Why didn't you ring?"

As I hugged her, over her shoulder I glimpsed a young man sitting on the rail of one of the pens. He appeared to be watching us intently but was too far away for me to see him clearly. I took him for one of the farmworkers - he'd been dressed in rough trousers bound at the bottom with twine, and an old flannel shirt. He must have been sweating in the summer's heat. Guy should rake him over the coals for slacking - I'd mention it to him.

Clair was peering at him too, as if she recognized him. She sat back in her garden chair and smiled.

Angela kissed Claire's cheek, ruffling her hair, an intimacy reserved for her alone.

"Hello, Auntie Claire. How are you?"

"Well, I suppose, for someone as old as Aidafell," she said with a straight face.

Joe and Guy rejoined us, looking scrubbed and healthy in the way of men who spend the best part of their waking hours outdoors.

"I'll put the kettle on," said Claire, "Sarah's gone home but I think she was baking this morning. Won't be long."

"Sarah Sutcliffe's immortal," I said to Angela, "but thank the Lord she got married and retired from the entertainment business."

Angela, who'd known Sarah her whole life, laughed out loud but was brought up short by a loud crash and bang, followed by a deathly silence as the earth seemed to stand still.

Angela was a graceful twenty-two year old when Joe's mother and my dearest friend died peacefully in his arms on the kitchen floor at Bythwaite..

It was the second time I'd seen Molly. Of course, no-one saw her but Angela and me. My grandmother stood over Claire's empty mortal shell and raised her by the hand until they stood side by side. Grace Kelly and the Dumfries enchantress.

By Nethershaw standards it was a lavish funeral.

Defying convention, Joe saw to it that his mother and father were interred side by side. As Claire had understood Molly's wishes, so my brother understood his mother's.

If the town's folk wondered why Claire Graham and her brother-in-law were in adjoining plots no-one said anything. Even the gossips 'kept their gobs zipped', most likely for fear of Deirdra.

The lady herself must have raided every flower shop and allotment from Nethershaw to Kendal for the flowers. The whole church was decked out and she made us all wear wild-flower button-holes. That's what Claire would have loved best, she said. I swear the woman cried for four days solid.

I was surprised how many people turned out to see the cortege pass. Both Sean and Paul had married locally and they came with their entire families, in-laws and *their* families and children as well, until it seemed that the whole of the town was connected in some way to the mourning.

Robbie wasn't there. He was working in New York as a photographer which considering he'd got 't'lass from t'chemist in't family way', his mother thought he'd led 'a bloody charmed life, the bastard'. But he was there to pay his respects to the lady he'd come to know as Auntie Claire within the week, sad and alone in his grief.

Deidra had a standing order with the local florist to deck Claire's grave with fresh flowers weekly. We all offered to contribute but she insisted it was her treat, as if she was buying her an ice cream.

Halfway through the service, while the whole congregation were sniffing into soggy hankies, Angela dug me in the ribs and nodded at the door.

"Do you see them?"

All I saw were mote-filled multi-hued shadows from the stained glass windows, but later she whispered for just the two of us to hear:

"There's the man from Auntie Claire's photograph too. Perhaps now they're all together we won't see them again."

She smiled to herself as a beautiful red butterfly lighted on her finger, and opened and closed its wings before fluttering away.

Witch Stones

Witch Stones

Characters

Joseph Graham

Mary 'Molly' Carrick Graham

Parents of Richard and Robert Graham

Robert Graham

Sheep farmer of Fairview, a small-holding near Nether-shaw in Westmoreland

Moira Armstrong Graham

Robert's deceased wife

Ellen Graham

Margaret /Maggie/Meg Graham

John 'Johnny' Graham

Children of Robert and Moira Graham

Richard 'Dick' Graham

Brother of Robert Graham. Owner of Bythwaite Farm near the hamlet of Beckton

Claire Armstrong Graham

Wife of Dick

Joseph 'Joe' Graham

Their son

Guy Greenwood

Life-long friend of Joe Graham

Joshua 'Josh' Greenwood

Guy's father, stakeholder tenant farmer for Dick Graham at Scarsdale Manor Farm.

Hugo Peter Mitford-Clarke Esq

Wealthy local magistrate and businessman, Owner of Luneside House near Nethershaw

Valerie Mitford-Clarke, his wife

Jennifer Mitford-Clarke, their daughter

Matthew 'Matt' Elliot

Gardener at Luneside House and Meg's helper on her allotment.

Ruth and Marjorie Elliot

Spinster aunts of Matthew

Inspector Fernside

Investigating Inspector of Police from Penrith

PC Robert 'Bobby' Ryder

Police constable resident in Nethershaw.

Reverend Timothy Robertshaw

Minister at the Methodist Chapel in Nethershaw

Tony Scarr, Dan Barber

Farm workers at Ghyll Howe Farm

Dermot O'Connor

Manager, Ghyll Howe Farm

Deidra his wife and great friend of Meg

Sean, Paul and Robin/Robbie, sons of Dermot and Deidra

Locations:

Fairview, Aidafell, Westmoreland

Smallholding owned by Robert and Moira Graham, and childhood home of their three children, Ellen, Margaret (Maggie or Meg) and John/Johnny

Nethershaw

A market town in Westmoreland

Kendal

A large town in Westmoreland

Penrith

Town, administrative center of Westmoreland police.

Coniston

A lakeside town where Joe and Guy purchase a property for rental.

Luneside House

Manor house, home of Hugo Mitford-Clarke, his wife Valerie and daughter Jennifer.

Ghyll Howe Farm

Meg Graham's farm, built up 'by the sweat of her brow from scratch'

Bythwaite Farm, Beckton

Home of Richard and Claire Graham and their son Joe

Beckton

Hamlet near Bythwaite Farm in Westmoreland

Scarsdale Manor Farm

Secluded farm in the fells above Beckton. Owned by Richard Graham but let to Joshua/Josh Greenwood as tenant and stakeholder.

The Seven Sisters

A mysterious Neolithic stone circle on a hilltop between Bythwaite and Scarsdale Manor Farm.

Witch Stones

Also available on Amazon from Lizzie Collins

The Ultimate Link series

Book One - Catch a Falling Star

Book Two - The Twinkle in Pa's Eye

Book Three - The Mountain Monk and Shadow Rider

The story of the fall from grace of an international rock star and his rescue by three strong, but very different women and friends who had loved him more over a life-time than he had ever imagined.

The Life and Times of Grace Harper Maxwell

The back-story of a fascinating and enigmatic character from the Ultimate Link series.

Bridie O' Neill and Cathal's Ghost

Adventures of a girl born into abject poverty in New York who discovers a whole new family, friends and romance in County Wicklow in Ireland.

Printed in Great Britain
by Amazon

30176661R00159